A Cowboy and his Secret Kiss

Sweet Contemporary Cowboy Romance,
Chestnut Ranch Romance, Book 7

Emmy Eugene

CHAPTER 1

B rian Gray sat on the end of the row, thinking that at least Darren and Sarena had splurged for comfortable seats. Darren had been living in the farmhouse at Fox Hollow Ranch for the last several months, but the house they'd been building had been finished last week.

After today's vow renewal, Brian would be staying with the other cowboys to help them move.

He didn't want to, just like he'd rather be anywhere but sitting in this chair—padded or not—on this deck. He hadn't trundled down the road to the farmhouse here for months, not that he'd done so much before either.

When he came to Fox Hollow, he only made it fifty feet down the dirt lane before he pulled over into the stand of trees that hid his truck from Serendipity's sisters. But he'd stopped doing that just before Christmas, when he'd finally told Seren that he couldn't keep sneaking around with her.

She'd actually seemed perplexed by him wanting to pick

her up at the front door. "I don't see why it matters," she'd said.

It mattered to Brian. When he'd asked her why she couldn't tell her sisters about their relationship—which had been seven weeks old at the time, and he still hadn't kissed her —she'd only blinked at him. Without a response, Brian had simply shaken his head and added, "Sorry, Seren. That doesn't work for me."

The problem was, the past six months hadn't really been working for him either.

Serendipity Adams currently sat several rows in front of him, her back tall and straight, her dark hair curled, clipped back, and cascading over her shoulders. Brian's fingers fisted just thinking about touching that hair. He wanted to cradle her face in his palm, lean toward her, and kiss her.

He hadn't stopped thinking about doing just that for the past eight months. Eight long months of torture from within his own mind. He hadn't been this hung up on Cassie, his ex-wife, and he couldn't figure out why the idea of being with Serendipity wouldn't stop tormenting him.

The pastor stood at the edge of the deck now, and the back door opened behind Brian. He turned and stood, along with the rest of the small crowd. If he could've gotten away with not coming to this, he would have stayed at Chestnut Ranch. As it was, he hadn't been able to figure out how to tell Darren —and by doing that, Sarena—that he couldn't sit on this padded chair and watch the vow renewal.

He shifted his feet as Darren came outside, wearing a dark suit, a pure black cowboy hat, and a wide smile. He extended his hand to someone still inside, and Sarena put her hand in his and came outside. The crowd sighed as a single unit, and Brian could admit that she was simply stunning in a white dress that went over her shoulders with thick straps and fell all the way to the ground in long waves of lace.

She didn't carry flowers, and all of her adornments were simple. Gold hoop earrings, and no other jewelry. She wore makeup, but not so much that she looked like a different person. Seren was a lot like that, with a fresh face that floated through Brian's mind every night before he fell asleep.

Sarena linked arms with Darren, and together, they walked down the center aisle while some frilly music played out of the house. They reached the front of the crowd and stood before the pastor.

Brian's throat scratched, and the air going down felt like the wrong thing to breathe. He managed to sit along with everyone else, and someone closed the door to silence the music. Once everyone was settled, Pastor Hamilton said, "Welcome to everyone here today to witness the vow renewal of Darren Dumond and Sarena Adams."

He continued to lead them through a very simple ceremony, which ended five minutes later when Sarena finished saying how much she loved Darren and always wanted to be with him.

The crowd stood again, clapping and cheering this time. Brian played his part, though he couldn't find a trace of happiness in his body. At least not for himself. He did smile for Darren and Sarena, who'd managed to stay married for three times as long as Brian had.

He wondered if he'd ever get married again. At only thirty-five, he didn't want to think about spending the next forty years by himself. Darren had gotten himself a dog last year, and Brian had followed in his footsteps.

His German shepherd had run out onto the ranch when Brian had arrived with Tomas and Aaron, and he wished he had Queen at his side to calm him. The dog had been training to enter the police force, but she'd failed one of the tests. Brian had paid a lot of money for her, but everyone thought he'd rescued her from the animal shelter.

They didn't ask where he'd gotten her, and he hadn't told them. That was his policy. If no one asked specifically, he didn't tell. Then he didn't have to lie, and the policy had served him well for a long time.

"Okay," Sorrell said. Brian looked at the third Adams sister. "We're having brunch out here before we all help the happy couple move into their new home. I just need a few minutes to get it all set up." She turned to the two cowboys who worked at Fox Hollow, and the three of them hurried down the aisle and into the house.

The music spilled out the open doorway again, and Theo and Phillip set up two long tables that Sorrell proceeded to fill with flutes of champagne and orange juice, croissants, salmon and cream cheese bagel sliders, fresh fruit, and caramelized onion mini quiches.

Brian's mouth watered, but he hung back, because Seren flitted around the tables too, putting out silverware, plates, and napkins. He couldn't help watching her, and if she felt the weight of his gaze on her face, she never acknowledged it.

"All right," Sarena said, taking up a position in front of the tables and raising both arms. Darren stepped to her side, the glow of happiness on his face so obvious. "Thank you all for coming, not only to the renewal but to help us move." She grinned out at everyone. "And a special thank you to Sorrell, who singlehandedly made this brunch for us."

Both she and Darren beamed at Sorrell, and Theo started the applause for her. Sorrell's face flushed, but her smile gave away how pleased she was.

"Okay, let's eat," she finally said, shooting a look at Theo and Phillip. Neither of them looked ashamed or embarrassed though, and in fact, Theo grinned at Sorrell in a way that told everyone exactly how he felt about her. Anyone looking, anyway, and Brian was always looking.

He felt like a silent observer everywhere he went, and he wondered if it was time for him to move on. He'd been at Chestnut Ranch for six years, and he'd spent a couple at another one just outside of Fredericksburg after his move from the Pacific Northwest.

One more glance at Serendipity, and Brian didn't want to move on. He wanted another chance with the tall, leggy brunette who'd somehow stolen his heart in a single second. Or maybe when she'd chased him down the lane to give him her number.

A number which he still had. A number he'd texted plenty of times in the past to ask her what time they could meet.

His hand immediately inched into his pocket, reaching for his phone. Maybe he could just text her now and ask her again.

His throat constricted, and he swallowed, trying to find

the courage he needed to send such a text. He should definitely do it before he ate, he knew that much. In fact, he wasn't sure how he'd chew and swallow at all until the text had been sent, and yet, he didn't quite know the words to use.

"You comin'?" Aaron asked, and Brian's hand slipped right out of his pocket.

"Yeah," he said, following the other cowboy toward the tables near the house. Plenty of others had already gotten their food, and with the small crowd, it hadn't taken long. In front of him, Aaron picked up a plate and proceeded to put one of everything on it. Brian had heard about Sorrell's excellent skills in the kitchen from Seren, and he should want one of everything too.

He used the delicate tongs and tiny forks to do the same as Aaron, finally taking a mimosa to occupy his other hand. Then he couldn't text Seren, who'd taken her plate of food to one of the tables that someone had put candles and tablecloths on at some point. Brian hadn't seen when, and he wondered how long he'd stood there with his hand in his pocket, trying to decide if he could text Seren or not.

Still following Aaron, he sat at another table and put down his plate and drink. He didn't waste any time now as he swiftly reached for his phone and pulled it from his pocket. He swiped and tapped, typing out Seren's name and getting the message started.

I miss you. I'd love to maybe see if we can try again. Later today after Darren and Sarena are moved? Same spot as usual?

He stared at the words, wondering if they were too desperate. To make matters worse, he added *Tell me what time, and I'll be there*, and sent the whole thing. He wasn't sure if Seren had her phone with her, and he kept his eyes on her back as he picked up his quiche. At the table beside him, the Johnson brothers laughed loudly about something, and Brian knew he didn't want to leave Chestnut Ranch. He loved the land there, and he loved working with good men like them.

He wanted to talk to Seth about Serendipity, but he hadn't known how to bring it up. Seth had always been the brother to ask the most questions, but he'd been really distracted with the upcoming adoption he and Jenna were hoping would go through.

"This is amazing," he said, realizing what he'd just put in his mouth. The salty onions and creamy eggs melted in his mouth, and his appetite returned despite the silence of his phone. He'd just finished the delicious brunch when his phone buzzed.

"Just leave the dishes," Darren said in that moment. "We'll clean it all up later. We've got plenty of work for you to do." He laughed, and so did several others.

"Yeehaw!" Theo whooped, and that set off Rex, and then Griffin.

"Oh, boy," Aaron said, grinning. "He's got them going now."

"Boxes in the house," Darren said over the commotion. "We'll need the big muscles to move the furniture."

"So not you," Rex said, jostling Travis.

"Funny," Travis said back. "I'm pretty sure I'm stronger than you."

"Please," Rex said. "You don't even work the ranch anymore."

"I lift weights," Travis said. "And Porter is no lightweight." He grinned at Millie, his wife, who held their baby boy in her arms. He leaned over and kissed her adding, "You gonna head home, baby?"

"When Jenna goes," Millie said. "She's my ride."

Travis nodded, and he practically shoved Rex toward the back door. "Let's go, Strong Man. You can probably take the couch by yourself."

Rex said something in return, but the noise level had increased, and Brian couldn't hear what. He loved the relationship between the Johnson brothers, and how they'd always made him feel like part of them too. He missed his brother in that moment, as he hadn't spoken to Tom in a couple of months.

He made a mental note to call Tom, and he pulled out his phone to make the note physical. He couldn't keep his mental notes as straight as he once had, and time would slip away from him, and the next time he'd remember to call Tom would be late at night or while he was driving. Sometime when he couldn't do it, and then more days would pass.

The text notification at the top of the screen reminded him of the buzzing of his phone, and his heart vibrated along with it. His chest almost hurt as hope filled him. He pulled down from the top of his screen, and his breath caught in his throat.

Serendipity's name sat there, along with a short text. *4:30. I miss you too.*

Brian seized onto those words, and they echoed through his whole head. His ears, his mind, his chest. *I miss you too.*

"Are you going to stand there all day?" Seth asked, causing Brian to jump. He looked up and at Seth, who gazed at Brian's phone.

"No," Brian said, shoving his phone back into his pocket at the same time he stepped out of the doorway. "Sorry."

"Not a problem." Seth grinned at him. "But we better get a move on if you've got somewhere to be at four-thirty." He wore a glinting, knowing look in his eye as he grinned and stepped past Brian into the house.

Four-thirty. It seemed impossibly far away and yet way too close at the same time. "Yeah," he said. "We better."

CHAPTER 2

Serendipity Adams stuck to the lighter boxes as the activity around the farmhouse amped up. She could carry more, but there was no need as Darren had brought all of the cowboys from Chestnut Ranch to help with moving day.

Moving day.

She couldn't believe her sister was moving out. Seren reminded herself that Sarena wasn't going very far. Two hundred yards, as she'd been telling Sorrell for the past few weeks. Sorrell, the middle sister, was definitely having a harder time with their oldest sister's departure from the farmhouse than anyone else.

Seren bent to pick up another box, a groan coming out of her mouth. "This one's heavy," she said, though she wasn't talking to anyone specific.

"Let me."

Seren knew that voice. That voice haunted her when she

woke up each morning and followed her around while she led groups to the top of Enchantment Rock.

She managed to turn her head to look at Brian Gray, the handsome cowboy she'd started seeing last fall. Maybe it was winter, though Seren didn't think winter's cold kiss ever truly came to the Texas Hill Country. She absorbed the strong lines of his jaw, which sported a trim, neat, and very sexy beard in the brownish-blond hair that covered Brian's head too.

He had a lot of hair, and Seren never had touched it. *What a shame,* she thought to herself as they continued to stare at one another.

He'd texted her a couple of hours ago and then promptly gotten to work moving the bed, the new couches Darren and Sarena had bought for their new house, and more after she'd responded to his message. He hadn't said anything back, and Seren told herself again that he didn't need to.

He'd asked to see her, and she'd agreed. Given him a time. They'd never done more than that before unless they had something fun or important to say to one another.

Brian's dark eyes devoured her, and Seren couldn't believe she hadn't allowed herself to kiss him last time. He'd wanted to kiss her. He'd even tried once before she'd told him she wasn't ready.

The truth was, Seren might never be ready to kiss a man like Brian Gray. She'd never kissed someone like him before, and as soon as his lips touched hers, he'd know that. In fact, Seren had only kissed two other men before, and neither of them were all that memorable.

Besides the fact that the last cowboy who'd taken his hat

off to kiss her had laughed afterward. That had definitely burned itself into her memory, and her throat tightened at the nearness of Brian.

The scent of his cologne entered her nose, and he called to her in a way no one else ever had. He'd been working for a while in the June heat, and he reached up and removed his hat. Her heart went into overdrive, her pulse moving through her ribcage and down into her organs.

He wiped his forehead with a towel and reseated his hat. Of course he wasn't going to kiss her right now. The very idea was absolutely ridiculous.

"I can get it," he said. "Your sister said there were a few boxes in here with books." He lifted the box as if it held feathers and added, "Yep, this is one of those." He nodded at her and turned around.

She watched him walk away, a flush of heat moving through her whole body. His biceps strained, so the box actually was heavy. But wow. Seren sure did like the way his jeans hung off his hips and the way his dark gray T-shirt strained across his wide shoulders.

All of the cowboys had changed after the vow renewal and following brunch. It had been a wonderful ceremony, and Seren was glad Sarena had gotten the event she wanted. She'd bought another dress for this ceremony, though she'd purchased one for the fake wedding they'd held at Fox Hollow last October.

Darren, apparently, had a lot of money. He'd funded the new house two hundred yards down the lane too, which he'd also paid to extend to their front driveway. They hadn't removed any trees, as the land conservation was important to Sarena—and to Seren too.

"Almost done in here," Darren said, entering the office where Seren still stood, mute. He bent and picked up another box, groaning under the weight of it. "Why did she put so much in one box?" He gave Seren a dark look and followed Brian out of the room and then the house.

With only a couple of boxes left, and with Seren assuming they also held books, she decided to leave them there for the cowboys to take. She went down the hall and into the back of the house, where the kitchen and living room spread before her.

Sorrell worked there, rinsing dishes and setting them in the dishwasher. Darren had replaced that too, for Sorrell's birthday. Her sister had burst into tears and hung onto his neck while she hugged him. Theo had brought her flowers and her favorite hazelnut chocolates and asked her to dinner.

Seren wasn't sure if her sister had said no or not, but she knew the date hadn't happened yet. She'd always believed it would, but she was starting to have her doubts. At the same time, she'd thought she'd ruined whatever chance she and Brian had, but he'd still texted.

Theo himself walked through the back door at that moment, and said, "Sorrell, this is all there is." He carried dishes and glasses in both hands and walked them over to the sink where Sorrell stood. She was the lightest of the Adams sisters, with hair the color of taupe that she actually lightened with an at-home dye kit. Her eyes bore the color of milk chocolate cocoa, and she glanced at Theo as he set the clinking dishes next to the sink.

"Thank you, Theo," she said, and Seren knew she'd been crying.

Thankfully, Theo stayed at her side, even putting his hand on her lower back as they worked at the sink together. Seren felt frozen to the spot as she watched them. She'd seen her mother and father doing a dance like this before, but it had been a very long time. She remembered the feeling of love and comfort as her father had looked at her mother, a glow of adoration on his face.

If Seren could see Theo's face, she was sure she'd see that same emotion on his face. She was glad he was there for Sorrell, as Seren didn't really understand her sister's emotions. Sometimes Seren felt like she was broken, as she didn't seem to think or feel things the same way other women did.

Because of that, she didn't have a whole lot of female friends. She barely had any friends at all. She'd always been close to her sisters, and for her, that was all she'd needed.

She was friends with a co-worker, Meg, though they didn't exactly have friendly lunches or go to movies outside of their work at the Enchantment Rock State Park.

Koda, Darren's dog came through the back door too, his tongue lolling out of his mouth. Seren sprang into action to get the canine something to drink. She'd found the presence of Koda at the farmhouse soothing and wanted. They'd never had a dog that lived inside and slept on the couch or the beds.

Koda did, though. If he got too dirty outside on the ranch with either Darren or Sarena, Darren just hosed him down on the back deck and then toweled him off before he let him inside. Seren loved the golden retriever, and she'd taken him to work with her several times, keeping him on the leash as she led her groups up the rock. Koda was a Rockstar, and he did whatever Seren told him to do.

She'd been seriously considering getting a dog of her own, after Sarena and Darren moved and took Koda with them.

"Hey, Koda," she said to the animal. He wore a smiling face, as he always did, and Seren brushed the dust from his long, golden hair. "Let me get you a drink."

Theo and Sorrell shifted, but Seren said, "I'll get a bottle."

"He's a dog," Sorrell said. "He doesn't need bottled water."

Seren ignored her, because of course Koda needed bottled water. She took two bottles out of the fridge and opened them to pour into the clean bowl she then collected from the cupboard.

"Don't use a bowl we eat out of," Sorrell said while Theo started chuckling.

"I'll wash it," Seren said, though she wouldn't. She'd load it into the dishwasher, though, if there was room after Sorrell got all the brunch dishes inside.

"You will not," Sorrell said, but Seren still set it on the floor and poured the two bottles of water into it.

A German shepherd came trotting inside the house too, and Seren paused at the magnificent sight of him. The dog had a glorious fawny coat, with all the characteristic black markings of a purebred German shepherd. "Oh, hello," she said. "Who are you?"

"That's Brian's dog," Theo said over his shoulder. "Her name's Queen."

Seren's heart bumped around inside her chest, quickly becoming dislodged as she bent down to greet the dog. "Come get something to drink, Queen."

Queen—and the dog clearly knew she was royalty. Brian probably treated her like one too, as she clearly came inside houses. She probably slept in his bed and on his couches too. *Lucky dog*, she thought, surprised at the thought. She'd barely kissed a man. Doing more than that...Seren gasped for a breath of the right substance to breathe.

The shepherd let her stroke her face and then she bent down and drank with Koda. The two of them lapped with their big tongues until they were satisfied, and then they both went over to the couches in the living room and jumped up on the biggest ones.

Seren loved them both so much, and she almost wished she didn't. She should want to spend her time with people she could speak with, not dogs who could keep her feet warm while she ate ice cream and rested her muscles from her long day at work.

To her right, Sorrell giggled, drawing Seren's attention. She looked at her and Theo again, a new idea growing and growing. The seed had been planted months ago, when Sarena, in another of her meddling attempts, had confronted Sorrell about going out with Theo.

She'd questioned Seren relentlessly about where she went at night too, and Seren had managed to put her off and say she wasn't sneaking around with anyone. She wasn't. Brian picked her up at the visitor's center or down the lane, and they went to dinner and movies. Just because it didn't happen in Chestnut Springs didn't mean she was sneaking.

She was keeping Brian a secret, because Sorrell had made her promise not to let a cowboy steal her heart and give it back to her in pieces. Seren had never had anyone, cowboy or not, come knocking on her door, anxious for a date, so she'd agreed. She'd been able to keep the promise for years. Almost a decade. It had been easy, because the disastrous kiss with the Laughing Cowboy had happened a couple of months before.

She hadn't told anyone about it, not even her sisters. It was bad enough that Pierce's friends all knew. Everyone at the party knew, too. That she'd had to live through the humiliation the first time. She couldn't stand the thought of telling the story to anyone, least of all Sorrell, who would expect Seren to cry so she could stroke her hair and reiterate the fact that all cowboys had trouble running through their veins.

Seren hadn't cried. Not even once. Not over Pierce Thrombey. He'd left town a couple of years later, and Seren lived and worked far enough from Chestnut Springs that she hadn't had to work too hard to steer clear of him or his friends.

Seren couldn't remember the last time she'd cried at all.

She tore her eyes from Sorrell and Theo, still dancing around each other in front of the sink. "I'm going to go shower," she said. "Get this dust and sweat off me."

"Okay," Sorrell said. "It was a great ceremony, wasn't it?"

Seren put a bright smile on her face, because she agreed with her sister. "Yes," she said. "It was."

"I still can't believe she's not going to come down the hall in the morning, ready for her coffee." She sniffled, and Seren took that as her cue to get out of there. As she walked away, Theo said something in a low voice, and Seren hoped Sorrell would just let go already.

Let go, and let herself go out with Theo. Let go, and let herself fall all the way in love with him.

Then maybe Seren could bring Brian out of the shadows and date him openly, the way he wanted.

Maybe, she thought, quickly switching her thoughts to a prayer. *Please, Dear Lord. If Sorrell can get out of her own way, then I can date Brian the right way. Please.*

She didn't want to hurt him. In fact, the idea of that made her physically ill. She may not think herself all that emotional, but she was considerate. She'd already hurt him, and Seren couldn't stand the thought of doing it again.

"Maybe you shouldn't meet him this afternoon." Seren showered quickly without washing her hair. She got herself properly deodorized and dressed in a cute pair of black shorts and a white tank top. Though she rarely wore sandals around the ranch due to the amount of dust, today, she slipped on a strappy pair of flat sandals. She never wore heels, as she was already the tallest Adams sister.

With Brian, she could wear the extra height, because he stood much taller than her that heels wouldn't even touch. She didn't even own heels though, and she would never be able to walk in them. Since she'd already made a fool of herself in front of Brian—more than once—she was sticking to the flat sandals.

She'd thought about how she'd run after his truck after they'd met for the first time. She'd seen him around before, but they'd truly met when he'd come to help Darren move into the farmhouse.

Then she'd rejected his kiss, which only added another layer of embarrassment. Then she'd refused to let him come to the door to pick her up. Wouldn't go out with him unless they ate in another town. When he'd finally broken up with her, Seren had actually been relieved. Then she didn't have to keep adding more guilt to her gut. More embarrassment to what she already carried on a daily basis.

But maybe...

At four o'clock, the house seemed to be empty. Both dogs were gone, which meant Brian and Darren had come to get them at some point while she'd been hiding in her bedroom. She thought the farmhouse would probably feel and be a lot emptier now that Sarena and Darren and Koda didn't live here anymore. She clenched her teeth and stuffed her feelings back down into her stomach. She would be okay. Sarena deserved a home of her own, with the husband she loved. They wanted a family, and they needed a place of their own to raise that family.

Seren opted to walk down the dirt lane to the alcove of trees where she and Brian had met over the weeks they'd been seeing each other. She'd never arrived first, but she did today. Maybe things would be different this time.

You have to do something different to get a different result, she thought, unsurprised when she heard the rumble of an engine only a few minutes after she'd arrived.

Sure enough, Brian pulled his shiny, white truck around the corner a moment later. She tucked her hands in her back pockets and stayed out of the way while he parked. He got out, and still Seren felt like she was standing on wooden legs.

"Hey," he said, closing the door behind him.

The sun shone down, nice and warm, and Seren's nerves fired harshly. "Hey."

"So, um, do you want to go for a walk? Or should we stay here?" He looked around at the fully leafed trees, a smile crossing his face. "It looks different now that it's summer." When he met her gaze again, he kept the smile on his face.

"Let's stay here," Seren said, pushing her anxiety back. *Do something different.*

"All right." Brian nodded toward the back of his truck, where they'd sat and talked in the past. Before he could take too many steps, Seren darted in front of him. "Oh."

She looked into those eyes she liked so much, reaching up slowly. She traced her fingertips down the side of his face, that beard even more beautiful against her skin than she'd imagined.

Brian pulled in a slow breath, and Seren looked into his eyes. She wanted to ask him if he'd laugh. Or if he still wanted to kiss her. By the look in his eye, he did.

Because of that, Seren didn't waste another second. She tipped up onto her toes as she curled her other hand around the back of his neck, her fingers seeking out and finding that thick hair she'd dreamt about.

"Serendipity," he whispered, but she didn't know what to say. She had nothing to say. Her eyes drifted closed as Brian moved. He clearly knew what he was doing when it came to kissing a woman, because he put one hand on her waist while simultaneously using the other to remove his cowboy hat.

He leaned down and met her mouth with his, finishing the task she'd started. Seren sucked in a breath, her pulse positively pounding now. As if it hadn't been before. She had no idea what she was doing, but Brian obviously did. She felt treasured and adored as he kissed her and kept her close to him.

So Seren did what she hoped Sorrell would—she let go. She let go, and she enjoyed the way Brian kissed her. Wow, how he kissed her...

CHAPTER 3

Brian had been fantasizing about this moment for a very long time. Had he known Seren would kiss him the moment they got back together, he'd have texted her many days ago. She tasted like a hint of mint, and Brian simply could not get enough of her.

He got to feel that hair between his fingers, and his heart pounded in a way it hadn't before. He kissed her for probably too long, and by the time he got control of himself and broke their connection, he could barely breathe.

"Wow," he whispered, sliding his hands down her back to her waist, where he kept her right in his arms.

"Wow?" Seren leaned back, though she didn't step away. "Really?"

Brian opened his eyes and looked at her. So much wow, he wanted to kiss her again right then. His heartbeat skipped now for an entirely new reason. She was questioning his reaction to kissing her. Did that mean she hadn't liked it?

Admittedly, he hadn't kissed a woman for a while, but he felt like he still knew how. "Yeah," he said. "I don't think it's a secret that I've been wanting to do that for a while."

She shook her head, a small smile lighting her face. "No, I guess not. I just..." She looked away, and Brian let her step away too. She wore a pair of black shorts that went halfway down her thigh with a white tank top, leaving plenty of skin for him to admire. She worked outside, and he imagined her job at Enchantment Rock to be a lot like his at Chestnut Ranch—hardly ever a moment to sit down and relax.

Because of that, she had long, toned legs, and slender arms. Everything about Seren was thin, but she exuded a power from her core that he really admired.

"What?" he asked, stepping over and lacing his fingers through hers.

"The last man I kissed laughed afterward."

Brian could only blink. No wonder she hadn't been ready before. "I can't imagine why," he said gently. "I really enjoyed it."

She turned and looked at him, hope in those gorgeous, midnight eyes. "Really?"

To answer her question, he simply leaned down and kissed her again. Her fingers slid up the side of his face, and he felt the moment she released her tension and relaxed into the kiss. Only a second later, he pulled back. "Really."

Seren licked her lips and opened her eyes. "Do you want to go get a cinnamon roll or something?"

"Sure," he said, and he walked over to the passenger door and opened it for her. Once she'd climbed up, he rounded the front of the truck, coaching himself not to act too over-eager. There was still plenty to work out between the two of them.

He got behind the wheel and buckled up. "It was a great ceremony, wasn't it?"

"Yes," Seren said, her focus out the window. Brian had always been able to tell her mood by whether she'd look at him or not. While she may have kissed him, she was in a quiet mood, and he decided he didn't mind.

He went down the dirt lane and turned right onto the highway to make the twenty-minute drive to Chestnut Springs. "I have a question for you," he said.

"All right." She faced him, and Brian watched her try to put on a brave face.

"Are you—why couldn't we go out publicly before?" She never had told him, and Brian needed to make sure they were on the same page here, that amazing kiss notwithstanding. Last time, they hadn't even been reading the same book.

"Sorrell," she said. "I still need to talk to her."

Brian gave himself a few moments to riddle out what she'd said. "What does she have to do with us?" He glanced at her, and Seren frowned.

"She had this cowboy break her heart." She whooshed both hands over her lap. "Shattered it completely, and she made me promise that I wouldn't allow that to happen to me. So we made a vow to each other. Neither of us has really dated since."

Brian nodded, though there was a niggling part of him that said that wasn't the whole story. It sounded true, but it could be true and only one of the reasons she'd made him take her to restaurants forty-five minutes from the ranch where she lived.

He pulled into the line at the bakery, which wasn't as long as he'd seen it previously. They made cinnamon rolls as big as a man's head, and they started serving them warm at two o'clock. Sometimes by five, they were gone.

"Are you going to tell her?" Brian asked.

Seren looked at him, her smiling mask gone. She turned as the woman came to her window to take her order. She pressed the button to roll down the window, and she said, "We want one cinnamon roll." She looked at him. "Did you want your own?"

He shook his head, because his stomach had clenched tight. He'd been a fool to think so much had changed in the last six months. Seren hadn't changed. She was still who she was, and she wasn't going to let him drive all the way to the front door of the farmhouse at Fox Hollow Ranch.

The woman left to get their treat, and Brian didn't look at Seren as she rolled up the window. "Nothing's changed, has it?" he asked.

"I don't know, Brian. She's so unhappy about Sarena moving, and I...don't want to make her life harder."

"Why'd you agree to meet me then?" He did turn his head to look at her then. She'd said she missed him. "I'm not doing this if we can't see each other openly. I don't want to park down the lane, or drive to other towns for dinner. Nothing's changed for me in that regard."

Seren opened her mouth to say something but quickly closed it. The woman arrived with her cinnamon roll, and she had to knock on the window before Seren noticed. She didn't seem too happy with having to wait, as there were a lot of cars and trucks behind them.

Brian pulled away from the bakery and started back to Fox Hollow. What a waste of time. Not only that, but he'd just gotten over feeling like a fool for the last time he'd tried to make something work with Seren.

"My wife wasn't very interested in being with me," he said when she'd finished eating all she was going to eat and they were only a few minutes away from the ranch. "And I'm not interested in doing that again."

"You were married?" Seren asked.

"Yes," Brian said. "Once. A long time ago." He felt like the life he'd lived in Seattle belonged to another man, because in a lot of ways, it did. He made the turn and pulled into their secret meeting place. "I think this is where we leave it once again, Seren."

"Brian," she said, his name full of frustration. He felt like he was forcing her to do something she didn't want to do, and he didn't like that. But they were simply on two opposite sides of the fence here, and Brian was tired of trying to scale it.

Without another word, Seren slipped out of the truck, leaving her cinnamon roll behind.

Irritation and stupidity accompanied Brian back to Chestnut Ranch, where he parked in front of the cabin where he now lived alone, and went inside to let Queen out. "Should've stayed home with the dog," he muttered to himself.

She loved to train, and he chopped up some dried beef

liver he got from the butcher shop in town while she ducked out the back door. He went into the backyard with her and started working with the dog to bark when he wanted her to, and quiet on command.

"Enough," he said one more time, while Queen barked and barked. She quieted instantly, and he fed her the last of the liver. He sat on the bottom step, glad when Queen came right over and leaned into his leg. At least she wasn't embarrassed to be seen with him.

* * *

A couple of nights later, after another long day of work on the ranch and another training session with Queen, Brian remembered he'd made himself a note to call his brother. He set aside the guitar in his hands and reached for his phone.

"Hey," Tom said with half a laugh that was mostly smothered by a heavy sigh.

"Uh oh," Brian said, glad he'd called. "What's going on?"

"Oh, these boys," he said with plenty of disgust in his voice. "Remember that time we were fighting and Dad started yelling? 'Get in the car! Both of you in the car right now!'"

Brian chuckled, because he remembered. "I was so scared. I wasn't sure if he was going to beat us, or just yell some more, or what."

"Yeah, and he didn't do either of those things."

"It was the fear of the unknown."

"That's what my boys are missing," Tom said. "I feel like

doing what Dad did. Driving them all over the city and then letting them out, and saying, 'Find your way home, boys.'"

"Together," Brian said with Tom. They laughed then, and Brian was so glad he'd called. The last few days since kissing Seren had not been his best, and he was tired of the same old routine.

"We made it home, too," Brian said. "Together."

"Can you imagine if I did that?" Tom laughed again, heartily. "Seattle's not the same place it was when we were kids."

"Definitely not." Brian sighed too, and he realized too late that his brother would hear something in the sound. They may not talk every day, but they were all the other had, and they knew each other well.

"What's up with you?" Tom asked.

"Nothing," Brian said, not wanting to relive the humiliation. He should probably be thankful Seren had kept their relationship off the grid. Then he didn't have to tell anyone how he was doing. Seth and Russ Johnson didn't care as long as the work got done.

"Oh, come on," Tom said. "I just told you I'm ready to drive my kids into downtown Seattle and drop them off."

"Yeah, but they'll grow up and be best friends like us," Brian said.

"Not if you don't tell me what's going on. You hardly ever call for no reason."

"I called because you were about to load up your kids."

"Brian."

"It's embarrassing," he said.

"I know way more embarrassing things about you, I'm sure," Tom said. "So what have you got to lose?"

Brian thought for a moment, because his brother was probably right. "Okay, fine," he said. "I'm having this problem with this woman I like..."

CHAPTER 4

Seren waved good-bye to the group of people she'd just led to the top of the rock, ready to be out of the sun and heat. She'd get thirty-five minutes for lunch, and she'd gotten a couple of phone calls on the way down. By the time she ate half a sandwich, used the restroom, and reapplied sunscreen, she might have ten minutes to see who'd called.

She'd picked up the stargazer group for that night, because anything was better than sitting on the couch while Sorrell flirted with Theo. He'd asked her out at least a dozen times in the past, but she'd said no every time. By what Seren had seen, if he asked again, Sorrell would say yes.

Seren needed to talk to her sister about the promise they'd made to each other, but she didn't want to. She didn't want to admit that she had her eye on someone, because then Sarena would dance around and say she'd known Seren was sneaking around last winter.

Seren reminded herself that Sarena didn't live in the farmhouse anymore, and Seren didn't have to explain anything to her.

What she also didn't want to explain was that she had no idea how to be a girlfriend. She didn't know what women did for the men they liked, and she had no idea why on Earth Brian hadn't laughed at her immediately following the kiss.

Seren didn't have a self-confidence issue; that wasn't the problem. Her complete inexperience with dating and having a boyfriend made her nervous. Trying to figure out what Brian saw in her kept her up at night. No one had been interested before, and she wasn't sure how to hold the interest of a cowboy like Brian.

Her worries had created a barrier between them, and while Seren didn't normally have a problem telling people what she thought—Sorrell called her blunt—she didn't want to open her chest and lay out her personal fears for Brian to skewer.

She called her voicemail as she entered the visitor's center, the blow of air conditioning bringing relief to her super-heated skin. Russ Johnson's voice came on the line, wanting to know if she could take on a painting job at the homestead at Chestnut Ranch.

Seren hadn't taken on a side job for a while, and she did miss going over paint chips and envisioning what a room would look like when the sunlight poured through the windows. At the same time, it was the height of summer, and that meant tourists. Tourists meant Seren worked all the time, sometimes from dawn until dark.

"Serendipity," someone called, and she deleted the message as she looked toward the counter. Meg stood there, and she gestured for Seren to come over. Seren detoured toward the only friend she had who didn't share her last name.

"What's up?" She glanced at the woman standing there. She had three or four t-shirts on the counter, and Seren already knew what Meg needed.

"There's no tag on this," she said, handing her the pink t-shirt.

"I'll go get another tag." She bustled off to do that, though she didn't normally work the gift shop at the visitor's center. She picked up another medium-sized shirt and took it back to Meg.

"Thanks," Meg said, grinning at her. She tucked her dirty blonde hair and asked, "Are you going on lunch?"

"Yes. When's yours?"

"Fifteen minutes."

"Perfect," Seren said. "I'll still be back there." She scurried away, because if she didn't get off the floor, she'd be put to work. She wished she'd brought Koda to work, because then she'd have a reason to go back outside to a shady table to eat her lunch alone. She was once again reminded of her desire to spend time with animals over people, and she got out her lunch and set it on the short counter next to the fridge before ducking into the bathroom.

Her feet had just started to recover when Meg flopped into the chair across from Seren. "I'm beat. How were the groups this morning?"

"Good," she said, giving Meg a smile. "Plans tonight?"

Meg grinned, and that was all she needed to get going on the dating escapades she enjoyed. At the current moment, Meg was seeing a man named Walter, and Seren decided she better start paying attention when Meg talked about her dates. She could probably pick up a few pointers.

By the time Seren got home that night, she needed a shower and a lot of chocolate. Sorrell would hopefully have dinner wrapped under aluminum foil in a warm oven, as her sister loved to cook.

She opened the front door to a peal of laughter, and she wished she had the joy inside her to produce a sound like that. Right now, she found it difficult to smile at all, because she'd failed again to get a relationship with Brian off the ground. Even after kissing him, she hadn't been able to commit to bringing him home to her sisters.

Even now, the thought made her heart beat a little faster. She bent to take off her hiking boots, her feet getting instant relief. She went down the hall and into the back of the house, where the living room, dining room, and kitchen took up the wide, open space.

Theo and Sorrell sat at the kitchen table, and Sorrell looked toward the living room as Seren crossed through it. "She's home."

Theo looked at her too and got to his feet. "That's my cue to leave." He smiled at Seren, tipped his hat, and turned back to Sorrell. He said something to her in his deep, bass voice that was so low Seren couldn't hear it, and he eased out the back door a few seconds later.

"There's smothered pork chops in the oven," Sorrell said, turned from the door. She wouldn't meet Seren's eyes as she hurried into the kitchen and opened the oven. "I made mashed potatoes too."

Seren sat at the bar and let her sister serve her this ten p.m. dinner. Seren picked up her fork and kept her eyes on Sorrell until her sister asked, "What?"

"What?" Seren repeated. "You and Theo?"

"He hasn't asked me out." She sighed as she came around the island, and when she sat on the stool next to Seren, she downright exhaled all the air out of her lungs.

"You'd say yes?" Seren put a bite of pork chop and mashed potato in her mouth, surprised at Sorrell. She normally had to be convinced to do something, and she cried making the simplest decisions.

Sure enough, she sniffled next to Seren, who had no idea what she was crying about. She hadn't been particularly happy the past few days, but never once had the waterworks started. She ate her dinner while her sister wept quietly, and finally Seren said, "Well? Would you say yes?"

Sorrell shrugged. "It doesn't matter. He's not asking."

"Maybe you should ask him," Seren said, the idea bouncing around inside her mind too. Brian had reached out to her at the vow renewal. She hadn't heard from him since he'd driven away without even looking in his rear-view mirror.

Maybe she should ask him to take her to dinner. Or she'd take him.

"I can't ask him," Sorrell said miserably.

"Something to think about," Seren said. "What if

someone asked me out?" Seren tried to make her tone as casual as possible.

"Serendipity," Sorrell said, her tears instantly gone. "Keep talking."

"Look who's being blunt now."

Sorrell giggled as she nudged Seren with her shoulder. "Seriously. Who asked you out?"

"No one," Seren said. "I'm just thinking that if you go out with Theo, then maybe that promise we made to each other would be no big deal." She chanced a glance at Sorrell, whose wide eyes could see too much, in such a short time.

"Someone has asked you out," Sorrell said. "Who is it? Is he a cowboy? Someone at work?"

Seren got up and went to rinse her plate to put it in the dishwasher. Just because Sorrell would clean up after her didn't mean Seren had to take advantage of her. "Thanks for keeping my dinner warm, Sorrell," she said. "Sorry you had to be here alone tonight."

"I wasn't," Sorrell said. "I got Theo to stay with me." She smiled, but she looked tired. "I do have an early meeting in the morning, though, so I need to get to bed."

"Thanks for waiting up for me." Seren met her sister at the mouth of the hallway that led down to their bedrooms, and awkwardness descended on her. She loved her sisters, and she didn't ever want to do anything to upset them. She wasn't very touchy-feely, but Sorrell was, so her sister grabbed onto her and hugged her.

"Whoever it is," Sorrell said. "Maybe you should ask him."

"I'll ask him when you ask Theo."

"Then I guess neither one of us is going on a date any time soon." She preceded Seren down the hall, and Seren continued into her own room to get ready for bed.

Before she laid down, she sent a quick text to Russ to say she'd call him in the morning and she listened to the other message she'd forgotten about.

She deleted it after only a couple of words, because she had no patience for telemarketers telling her that she'd need to call back and confirm her address so they could send her all the information about a tropical vacation she'd won.

"Tropical vacation," she scoffed. "What would that be like?" She closed her eyes, and Brian's face appeared behind her closed eyelids. With him there, she calmed and she finally fell asleep, thinking maybe she could just text him in the morning.

CHAPTER 5

Brian picked up the ball and threw it for Queen again. "Get it," he told her, and she went bounding through the long grass at the edge of his yard. She was a very good dog, because she'd been trained to work until she achieved the goal.

She barked as she looked, and Brian liked watching her joy as she searched. She barked, dove, and came trotting back to him with the bright orange ball in her mouth. She dropped it at his feet and sat, and Brian gave Queen a bit of liver.

"All right, girl," he said. "I have to get over to the homestead." He went up the back steps and filled a big bowl with ice and water. The German shepherd lapped noisily as he left through the front door.

He drove the half-mile to the homestead, because the evenings in June could fry a man if he wasn't careful. Russ's big black truck sat in the driveway, but so did a load of flooring covered by a blue tarp.

Russ and Janelle had been planning a remodel at the homestead for the past couple of weeks, and just that morning, Seth had asked Brian to oversee it. Russ ran the ranch while Seth had transitioned over to the rescue dog operation, and Brian did whatever the Johnson brothers asked.

So if Seth wanted Brian to keep the remodel on track, he'd do it. He parked and walked up the sidewalk to the ten-foot wide front porch. He rang the doorbell, and Russ opened the door several seconds later. The scent of chocolate came with him, and Brian's night just got a whole lot better.

"Come in," Russ said with a smile. "Kelly's got double fudge brownies on the counter for you."

Brian's mouth watered, because Russ's step-daughter was an excellent baker, even though she was only twelve. "There better be ice cream too," Brian said, grinning as he stepped inside.

"There is," Janelle said as she came through the wide doorway, wiping her hands on a dishtowel. "Hey, Brian."

"Evening, ma'am," he said, tipping his hat. For the first time in a while, he felt like a real Texas cowboy. If Russ and Janelle had ever suspected he'd come from somewhere else, they wouldn't know it from his perfect Texas accent.

"Thanks for agreeing to take this on," Russ said. "We've got so much going on with the ranch, and Janelle's office is swamped." He led the way through the arched doorway, past the staircase that went up, and into the kitchen.

Kelly set a container of ice cream on the counter and smiled at him. "Evening, Brian," she drawled, and her accent was better than his.

"Caramel double fudge?" he asked, peering at the brownies.

"That's right." She opened a drawer and took out a knife. "Are we having brownies now, Mom?"

"Sure," she said, going to the kitchen table and opening a binder. "We can eat while we go over a few things."

Brian accepted the bowl of brownies and ice cream and joined Russ and Janelle at the table. She had three binders, actually, and Brian thought he might need another bowl of sweets to make it through this night.

He took a bite, the sugar giving him a renewed determination to do whatever Russ and Janelle wanted.

"Okay," Janelle said. "We've met with the interior designer a few times, and we've got fabrics and rugs ordered." She indicated the blues and grays and splashes of yellow in one binder. "The flooring is ordered and in the driveway."

"Too bad Millie's not at the furniture store anymore," Russ said. "Because we could've used that discount."

Brian glanced at him, wondering if Janelle would contradict him. All the Johnsons were billionaires, Brian knew that. Russ could afford to buy the whole furniture store and have plenty of money left over.

Janelle rolled her eyes, and Brian took another bite of his treat. "We got everything ordered," she said, turning the page.

Brian had overseen construction projects on the ranch he'd worked outside Fredericksburg, and he knew the timeline. "Demo day on Monday," he said, looking at her timeline. "Then the cabinets come in. The new, energy-efficient windows. The floors. Finally, the paint, and then you can load it with furnishings and rugs and curtains."

"How long?" Russ asked.

"A few weeks," Brian said. "You guys have done all the hard work already."

Janelle turned the page and sighed. "Almost. We just have to pick the paint color." She twisted toward Russ. "Is Serendipity coming over tonight?"

Brian dropped his spoon into his bowl, and it clanged against the bottom of it. He stood up quickly and returned to the kitchen.

"Yep," Russ said. "She said she'd help with the color."

"You can't influence her," Janelle said.

Brian couldn't be here when Seren showed up. He'd forgotten that she did house painting jobs on the side, and he scooped himself more brownies and ice cream, trying to figure out how to get out of this homestead as soon as possible.

If she saw him there, she'd bolt, and then Russ and Janelle would have questions. They'd also be out of a painter, which they needed. He finished another bowl of ice cream and brownies while Russ and Janelle argued over paint color.

The doorbell rang, and Brian nearly dropped his bowl.

"That'll be her," Janelle said, practically prancing out of the kitchen to get the door. Brian's throat narrowed, but he managed to put his bowl in the sink without shattering it.

Two female voices came closer, and Brian wanted to melt into the floor when Seren entered the kitchen behind Janelle. She wore a smile, a pair of cutoff jeans, and a blue t-shirt with a picture of Enchantment Rock on it. He knew what those lips felt like against his, and he couldn't stop the idea of kissing her again from running rampant through his mind.

"You know Brian Gray?" Janelle asked, pointing at Brian as if Seren hadn't already seen him. The smile fell off her face, and she crossed her arms as she nodded.

"Great," Janelle said, throwing a look at Brian. Seren had gone from hot to cold, and obviously Janelle had noticed. Russ picked up another brownie, so he didn't seem to feel any of the awkwardness.

"Okay, so we need your help choosing a paint color," Janelle said, picking up a stack of paint chips.

"What color are you doing the cabinets?" Seren asked, ignoring Brian completely as she passed through the kitchen to the dining table.

"White."

"Bright white? Ivory? Ecru? Dark white?"

"Bright white." Janelle looked up, respect in her eyes. "The countertops are gray quartz. We're doing blues and grays and yellows in our window treatments and rugs and furniture." She went on to explain things, and Seren simply stood there.

"I need to measure," she said. "Are we doing the same color throughout the whole house? Just back here? Out in the front room? The upstairs?"

"Just down here," Russ said. "And the front room."

"No," Janelle said, throwing him a look. "The whole house. Upstairs too."

Russ didn't look happy about that, and Brian felt like he was getting smothered by being in the same room with Seren. She wouldn't look at him, and he had to get out of there.

"Excuse me," he said, his voice almost choking in his throat. He went toward the front door and right out it. The air wasn't cool and comforting the way he wished it was. It filled his lungs as if he'd breathed in thick, tomato soup. He braced himself against the railing and tried to breathe in through his nose.

Why was he so hung up on this woman? Every time he even thought of her, his pulse went nuts. Being in the same room with her and not being able to look her in the eye was torture. He didn't want to work on this project if she was going to be the painter.

He didn't have to do a lot of the work, but it was his job to make sure everyone had what they needed. He was the one who'd be calling to check on timelines, and he would have to step in to complete projects if necessary.

The homestead was easily six thousand square feet, and there was no way Seren could paint the whole thing by herself.

"She won't take the job," he muttered to himself. Not if she knew she'd have to deal with him. He hated that he was something for her to deal with at all, and a deep sense of unhappiness wound through him.

The front door burst open behind him, and Seren crossed the porch and practically flew down the steps.

Brian must really like basking in his own humiliation, because he went after her. "Seren," he said, but she kept going. His cowboy boots slapped the wooden stairs as he went down them, and he finally caught up to her at her sedan. "Just wait a second."

She spun back to him, her face carrying a hint of redness. "What?"

"I didn't know they'd called you to do the painting," he said. "I swear."

"It's fine," she said. "I can't do it anyway."

"You won't have to see me much. Don't let me be the reason you don't take the job."

"I don't have time," she said, her dark eyes flashing with fire.

"Seren—"

Her phone rang, and she turned away from him as she answered it. Brian just wanted to go home. He could shower the sweat off his body and get some food to go with the dessert he'd already eaten.

"No," Seren said. "I'm at the homestead at Chestnut." She looked up, panic in her eyes. "You're kidding."

Brian stayed close by, though he didn't know what he could do to help. He wasn't going to touch her, that was for sure.

"All right," Seren said. "I'll be home in a minute." She put her back to him, but he still heard her say, "All right, Sorrell. I heard you." The call ended, and she looked back at him. She lifted her chin, and Brian saw the brave, strong Seren he'd started to fall for.

"What's going on at your place?" he asked.

Her façade crumbled, and Seren burst into tears.

"Okay," Brian said, stepping into her and taking her into his arms. Surprisingly, she came, and she held tightly to him too. He shouldn't be so happy about whatever had brought her to this point, but the gentle sigh slipped through him anyway.

Seren didn't cry for long, though, and she stepped back. "Sorry." She wiped her eyes. "Sorrell just said the air conditioning is out at the farmhouse."

"That's not good."

She shook her head, her dark hair swinging with the movement. "She's calling someone, and I have to go."

"I could come look at it."

"You could?"

"I'm handy with some things," he said. "Might tide you over."

"I'll talk to her." She turned and opened the door, pausing to look back at him. "Will you tell Russ I'll be back tomorrow night?"

"Yes." Brian stayed where he was on the sidewalk as Seren got behind the wheel, her phone back at her ear. He watched her until he couldn't see her car anymore, and then he got in his truck too. He sent a quick text to Russ, telling him Seren would be back the next evening, and he looked up and out his windshield.

They were adults. He could clear out of the homestead when she came over to work. Plain and simple. Now, if he could stop thinking about kissing her, Brian might have a chance of living a normal life.

CHAPTER 6

Serendipity woke in the morning with a gallon of sweat gluing her back to the bedclothes. She sat up, disgusted, and pushed her sticky bangs off her forehead. She'd thought she could sleep in the farmhouse with the windows open and the fan blowing directly on her.

She'd been wrong.

Sarena had offered for her and Sorrell to come stay at her new house, where the AC worked, but neither Sorrell nor Seren had wanted to.

She did now, though. She would tonight, because she honestly could not wake up in a pool of her own sweat again.

As she showered, she remembered the humiliating experience from last night. Had she really sobbed into Brian's chest?

She had, and Seren struggled to remember the last time she'd cried like that. Years. Everything had just felt so hard in that moment. So hard. She felt like she had to carry the weight of the world on her shoulders all the time as it was. She had to wear a smile at work, no matter if she had whiny teenagers on her hike, or crying babies, or snapping parents. She had to be kind all the time, no matter what.

Then, when she got home, she had to make sure Sorrell was okay. Fragile, delicate Sorrell. There was no one watching out for Seren, and when her sister had called in a near-panic, already crying, about the air conditioner being out, Seren found she couldn't carry one more thing.

She'd broken, and right in front of the very last person she wanted to see her weaknesses. He'd added to the load, though, because he'd been at the homestead. Why he'd been there, Seren had discovered from Janelle after he'd left.

He's the project manager still rang in Seren's ears.

She'd determined not to take the job. She didn't need the money, though for a house that big—upstairs and down—it would be a few thousand dollars. *A few weeks of work too,* she told herself as she finally started to cool off in the semi-warm shower spray.

Seren would have to paint the house around her day job at Enchantment Rock, and while she'd done projects like that before, they always meant sixteen or seventeen-hour work days.

She'd told Russ and Janelle she needed to run home and get her tool that would measure with a laser beam, and she'd be back to measure the surface area on the walls.

She'd never made it back over to Chestnut Ranch. She'd go tonight after work, because now she needed the money to replace the air conditioner.

Once she'd showered and dressed, she was already sweating

again. She pulled her damp hair into a ponytail, though it would get a bump, and went into the kitchen. There was no way she could force herself to drink hot coffee this morning, and bless Sorrell, she'd put a container of iced tea on the countertop, along with a note that read, *We're sleeping at Sarena's tonight.*

"Yes, we are," Seren muttered as she got out a glass and filled it with tea.

When she went out the front door, Koda came trotting toward her, and she caught sight of Darren and Sarena walking down the lane hand-in-hand. A brief flash zipped through her mind, and Seren could see herself doing that exact thing with Brian.

"Can I take him to work?" she called, indicating the dog.

Darren looked at her and raised his hand. "Yep. Tire him out, please."

Seren grinned and ran back inside to get Koda's leash, as well as the hiking cup she'd bought just for him. It had a flexible silicone piece attached to the top of it, and she could pour the water into that and let him lap it up, then smooth it down and fit it in her pack.

Outside again, she told Koda, "Come on, boy. Let's go hiking."

"Sorrell said the house got really hot last night," Sarena said, as she and Darren had drawn close to the farmhouse.

"Yes," Seren said. "Sorry, I'm so late. Are we okay to sleep at your place tonight?"

"Sure," Darren said while Sarena nodded.

"We'll talk about the air conditioner then," she added.

"Okay," Seren said. "Gotta run. See you tonight." As she drove down the dirt lane to the highway, she couldn't help thinking that she already had two tasks that evening, and all she wanted to do was crawl back in bed.

"No, you don't," she told herself. "Remember how hot that was?" She looked over to Koda, who just looked at her with big puppy dog eyes that begged her to scratch the ridges along his head.

She did, laughing when the canine closed his eyes as if in bliss.

Thoughts of Brian accompanied her all day, through every hike, through her breaks, and even through a very rousing lunchtime conversation with Meg. She loaded Koda into the car at the end of the day and blasted the air conditioning in her face.

The farmhouse felt one step away from the underworld in temperature, and sweat slid down the side of her face as she hurried to throw a few clothes in a bag, add a stick of deodorant, and get out of the house.

Koda lay outside on the back deck, and Seren thought it might actually be cooler out there than inside. A nice breeze blew, and the trees shaded the deck. "Come on," she told him, but he didn't even move. His eyes did slightly, tracking her as she passed.

She smiled and shook her head. "Are you tired? You need to go hiking with me more often." A special kind of exhaustion pulled through Seren too, though. It wasn't all physical either. The mental toll of thinking about Brian, and trying to decide what to do about Brian was definitely taxing. He never really seemed to give her any peace, and Seren wasn't sure what that meant.

She'd had crushes on other men in the past, but no one had ever dominated her thoughts like this. As she trudged toward Sarena and Darren's house, the bag in her hand growing heavier by the moment, she wondered what Brian saw in her.

Her stomach growled, but she ignored it. Inside the house, the blessed kiss of air conditioning met her skin, sending a sigh of relief through her. "I have to run over to Chestnut and measure for a job," she told her sisters, who both sat in the living room. Sorrell looked pale and tired, much how Seren felt.

Washed out and about to fade from view.

"You don't need to take that job," Sarena said, getting to her feet. She limped into the kitchen. "Darren said he'd pay for the air conditioner."

Seren balked at that instantly. "No, it's fine," she said, exchanging a glance with Sorrell. "We can do it."

They couldn't; not really. But with the job at Chestnut Ranch, she could earn a lot of money. "What did the tech say today?" she asked.

"He said we need a new compressor," Sorrell said, wiping one hand down her face. "And a whole new air conditioning unit. You know, the one outside?" She faced Seren, worry plainly on her face. "The farmhouse is old, but it's big. It's six thousand dollars."

Seren dropped her bag on the floor, and though it had shorts and T-shirts in it, it somehow made a clunking sound.

"Six thousand dollars?" She immediately started calculating how much she could charge Russ Johnson to paint the homestead.

"They're very expensive," Sorrell said. "Ours is twenty-four-years old, and they'll likely have to replace some of the HVAC system too."

Seren didn't know what to say, and she looked at Sarena. "Darren will pay for it," she said. "You guys know he's really rich, right?"

"Is he?" Seren said, seizing onto the information.

Sarena didn't look at her and stirred chocolate syrup into a glass of milk. "He has loads of money. Oil was found on a ranch he owned, and he sold it for billions." She finally looked up. "He won't even miss six thousand dollars."

"Let us think about it," Sorrell said. "You guys don't have to pay for everything for us. You have your own house and family to fund."

"Yeah," Seren said, though the idea of just letting Darren pay for the air conditioner appealed to her. "Brian said he could come look at it."

The moment she spoke, she knew she'd made a mistake. Sarena froze mid-stir, and Sorrell threw a look at Sarena and then focused back on Seren.

"Brian?" Sarena asked. "Why would he do that? Does he know anything about air conditioners?"

Seren felt rooted to the spot, and she mentally told herself to leave. "He said he's handy." She shrugged. "But Sorrell already had a guy come look at it. It's fine."

"Are you and Brian...you're friendly?" Sarena asked, finally stirring her chocolate milk again. It had to be well-combined by now, and the clinking noise of the spoon against the glass was driving Seren nuts.

"I have to run," she said. "Sorry. I'll be back later, and we can talk some more." As she drove over to Chestnut Ranch, she wondered if she and Sorrell could use Darren like a bank. Have him fund the air conditioner now, and they'd pay him back over time.

At a stop sign with no one else around, she quickly pulled out her phone and texted the idea to Sorrell.

I'll talk to him about it, she messaged back. *Good idea, Seren.*

Thanks.

And Sarena is not going to let the topic of Brian drop again, Sorrell added. *Just be ready.*

"Great," Seren muttered to herself, checking both ways again and then proceeding through the stop sign.

Maybe you should ask him. The idea revolved in her head, and she'd driven these roads out in the Hill Country so much, that she didn't have to use much brainpower to navigate them.

She drove past Seth and Jenna's house and onto Chestnut Ranch. It really was a beautiful piece of land, about four times as big as Fox Hollow. Their two properties butted up against one another on the west side of Chestnut, east of Fox Hollow, but Seren didn't work the ranch much and didn't really know what that boundary looked like.

She unconsciously slowed as she rounded the corner and saw the row of cowboy cabins. Three of them stood there, and a man sat on the steps of the first one, a guitar across his lap.

Brian.

His German shepherd lay at his feet, her tongue out as if she'd just had a good run.

Seren's first instinct was to pull over and talk to him. Perhaps he'd serenade her. She shook the ridiculous thought from her mind. He'd been kind to her last night, but nothing had changed between them. Not really.

"Unless you're willing to take him out of the shadows."

She pulled off the road on a whim, her heart pounding in her chest now. He'd looked up and seen her, and he was now leaning his guitar against the handrail before he stood.

"Do something different," she whispered to herself. "Ask him out." She unbuckled and got out of the car, mourning the loss of the air conditioning already. She told herself to be strong as she strode toward him, and Brian just watched her with those blue eyes that had been haunting her since the man had shown up on the doorstep of the farmhouse to help Darren.

"Hey," she said, bending down as Queen came over to her. Her heart warmed at the touch of the dog, and she really wished she got along as well with humans as she did animals.

"Hey."

She looked up from Queen's pretty face. "Are you going to the homestead tonight? Want to hitch a ride?"

He didn't give away a single thing about how he felt as he said, "Sure, okay."

Relief filled her, and Seren started thinking maybe they could have a third chance at a relationship. A real one, where she didn't sabotage it before it even started.

"Stay here, Queen," he told the dog, and he followed Seren to her car. He had to move the passenger seat all the way back to be able to get in, and then he cast her a quick look. "How's the air conditioning situation?"

"Not good," Seren said, quickly explaining what had to happen on the rest of the drive to the homestead.

"I'm sorry," he said as he got out. He looked up into the brutal sun-filled sky and added, "I can't imagine not having air conditioning right now."

"It's not great," Seren said. "Also, neither is that buttercup paint color Janelle wants, so I need you to help me persuade her away from it."

"Is that right?" He tossed her a grin as they walked up the sidewalk to the front door.

"Yes," Seren said. "It'll be way too warm in there, with all those windows in the back. They need a white with a gray or blue undertone. Green would be better than yellow, but not as good as blue."

"What's the one you want?" he asked.

"I haven't decided," she said. "But not buttercup." The door opened in the next moment, and Janelle stood there. Seren had fond feelings for the woman, as she'd helped Sarena keep the ranch last year.

"Hey," she said brightly. "Come on in." She stepped back and welcomed them to the homestead. "Did I hear you talking about buttercup?" She looked so hopeful, and Seren didn't want to burst her bubble.

"Maybe," Seren said evasively. "You got the other chips, though, right?"

"Yes," Janelle said. "You have to break our tie."

Seren was aware of the family battle they were having. Apparently, Russ and Kelly liked one color, and Janelle and Kadence another. Neither would come right out and say which one they liked best, but Seren knew Janelle's was buttercup by the incessant way she'd talked about it last night.

"Oh, I love coming here," Brian said in front of her. "Did you make this, Kelly?"

"Yes, sir," the girl said, and Seren finally made it into the kitchen to see the caramel and chocolate cheesecake sitting there. It was gorgeous with actual shards of caramel poking out of the top.

"Wow," she said, looking from the dessert to the girl who'd made it.

Brian looked at her with wide, hopeful eyes. "Can we eat before you start measuring?"

Seren thought she'd like some real food before all that sugar, but she couldn't say no to Brian when he wore the same kind of puppy dog pleading eyes that Koda had that morning.

She shook her head as she laughed, and said, "Sure."

CHAPTER 7

Brian wasn't sure what switch had flipped inside Seren, but he liked it. They both ate their cheesecake and chatted with Russ and Janelle, the atmosphere completely different tonight than last night.

He almost felt like one half of a couple, having dessert before dinner with their friends. He was friends with Russ and Janelle, but he worked for them too. He only came to the homestead when invited, and he spent more of his leisure time with Tomas and Aaron, as well as all the dogs Seth had on the ranch now.

Brian worked with the dogs in the run, the part of the ranch where the dogs that weren't up for adoption lived full-time. They had some social issues with other dogs, or had been so badly mistreated that they simply weren't fit to adopt out to families.

Brian loved working with them, because they reminded him of himself. Maybe a little broken, maybe a little snarly sometimes, and maybe he just wanted to lie in the shade and have people leave him alone.

At the same time, he didn't want to spend all of his time with the snarling, bad-tempered dogs. He didn't want to be one of those types of people either too.

He shot a look at Seren, but she seemed utterly relaxed tonight. She was gorgeous with all that dark hair spilling from the ponytail on top of her head, and she made his heart beat faster when she laughed at something Janelle said.

He thought about what Tom had told him. *Just try one more time.* Brian had been trying to figure out what that looked like and sounded like for the past twenty-four hours. He'd texted at the vow renewal. He'd been thinking about doing that.

He'd thought about driving right up to the door of the farmhouse too, but he feared if he did something like that, it would be akin to lighting a match and throwing it on a gas-soaked bridge. There'd be no rebuilding after that.

Tonight, he'd decided to sit on the front steps and play the guitar until he saw Seren drive by. He knew she was going to the homestead that night to measure the area so she could quote a price for Russ and then order the right amount of paint. He'd been planning to follow her a few minutes after that.

He'd never anticipated that she'd come to him, and as much surprise filled him now as had when she'd first pulled in behind his truck in front of his cabin. Queen had looked at him, and he'd set aside his guitar. He'd been praying for an opportunity to present itself, and he felt like the Lord had practically dumped Seren in his lap.

Ask her to dinner after you measure, he told himself. All she could say was no. He'd heard it from her before, actually, and it hadn't killed him. Driving away from her the other evening almost had though, and a healthy dose of humiliation drove through Brian.

He was not going to ask her out again. Hadn't he suffered enough at the hand of this woman? He shelved his thoughts and listened to Russ finish up a story about the ducks and geese on the ranch that Brian had heard before.

"Go on, now," Russ said once Janelle got up to retrieve her binders. "Ask him."

Brian put the last bite of cheesecake in his mouth, satisfied with the creamy texture and salty caramel. Kelly met his eye, and he saw nerves in the girl's expression. "What's up?" he asked.

"I've been, well, I want to go to this girl's horseback riding camp," she said, swallowing and shooting Russ a look. The cowboy nodded, and Kelly opened a drawer on the other side of the island. "I'm trying to earn half the money, and I made these dessert coupon books." She placed it on the counter in front of Brian.

He looked down at it, already knowing he was going to buy one. They weren't hand-drawn the way he and Tom had done for their mom for Mother's Day. Kelly had access to a computer and a color printer, and a tall cake sat on the cover, with bright pink frosting on it.

"You get to name the price," she said as he picked it up.

"There are a dozen desserts in it—ones I'm really good at—and you just have to text me which one you want, and I'll deliver it within two days' time."

Brian looked up, his love for this girl expanding. "This is great," he said. He picked up the booklet and opened it. "Oh, this cheesecake is in there." He glanced at Seren and showed her the book. "Kelly makes a great pecan pie too," he said. "I had it last Thanksgiving."

"Thank you, sir," she said.

"Can I see one?" Seren asked, and Brian thought he might fall in love with her right then. She smiled at Kelly as she took a second book and started leafing through it. "I didn't have those brownies last night, but they sure smelled good."

"I have some leftover," Kelly said, ducking over to the fridge and pulling out a bag of the caramel brownies Brian loved. They were in the booklet too, and he ate one while he browsed.

"I want three," Seren said. "Wait. Four. I want four." She beamed at Kelly and then switched her gaze to Brian.

He didn't want to be shown up by Seren, though he didn't think she had bones like that in her body. "I want one," he said. "And I think Tomas and Brian would like one. I'm assuming you're going to sell them to all of your uncles?" He glanced at Russ, who nodded.

Brian cocked his head. "Besides you, those are all my friends. So three for me."

"How much are they?" Seren asked, and Brian wanted to name some astronomical price. He could pay for Kelly's space camp from now until the end of time and still have money leftover.

"You name the price," Kelly said.

"How about a hundred bucks?" Brian asked. "Each. Do you have seven books?"

"I sure do." Kelly pulled them out of the drawer as Brian stood and pulled his wallet from his back pocket.

"Okay, let's see what I've got..." He flipped open the wallet. "I've only got...two-twenty. I can get you the rest tomorrow, and I'm paying for Seren's." He nodded toward her, not daring to look at her.

He suspected some of her tears from last night were due to a financial burden, and he wasn't about to let her pay four hundred dollars for dessert coupons. Not when he'd named the price. "Deal?"

"Deal," Kelly said, her whole face aglow now. She turned to Russ, who grinned with all the adoration of a loving father. "I got it all, Russ."

"You sure did." He embraced her, and Kelly skipped toward the stairs.

"All right," Janelle said. "Let's get down to business."

Seren tossed Brian a look he couldn't quite decipher as she moved over to the dining room table, where she started talking about undertones in white paint, and what the sunlight did to them. "You have so much yellow in here already," she said. "It's in the rugs, the curtains, the pictures. You don't want it on your walls. It'll be too warm, and you'll feel like you're one breath away from being on the surface of the sun all the time."

"I will?" Janelle asked.

"Trust me," Seren said. "You want a cool undertone. Now, Chantilly Lace is my favorite..." She continued talking about the "icier" colors, and with all the light that would come in the back windows late in the day—"the hottest part of the day, Janelle"—that they definitely wanted to go with something to cool down the room.

"I just don't want it to be clinical," Janelle said. "I work in an office that feels like a prison sometimes."

Seren nodded and looked at Janelle with all sincerity. "I get it. It's not going to feel cold. It's just going to balance out the other colors in your scheme, as well as play well with the sunlight. I promise." She smiled then, and Brian had to look away so his attraction to her wasn't quite so obvious.

"Want me to start measuring?" he asked while she continued the conversation about colors with Russ and Janelle.

"Sure." She handed him the tool she had, and Brian got to work. This thing was handy, as all he had to do was lay it flat against the wall and press a button that said "paint" and it would measure from where he stood to the next wall. He typed in the height of the ceiling, and the measuring laser kept track of all of it.

An hour later, he and Seren had the homestead measured. He'd eaten another piece of cheesecake that would probably keep him up at night, and the two of them left the homestead with their dessert booklets.

"You don't have to pay for mine," she said as they went down the steps.

"No," he said. "But I'm still going to. I named the price,

and that wasn't very fair for you." He wanted to tell her about his money, but at the same time, he'd kept it close and secretive for so long, he didn't want to get into the way he'd made his billions, or the life he'd had in Seattle.

They reached her car, and Seren quickly got the AC blowing. "So," she said with a sigh. "Did you eat too much cheesecake, or can you stomach having a real meal?"

Brian swung his attention toward her, his pulse pouncing into the back of his throat. "A real meal?" He sounded like he'd put a dozen marbles in his mouth, and he cleared his throat.

"Yeah," she said, backing up enough to turn around. "Dinner?" Her fingers clenched the wheel. "Let's go to dinner." She started driving down the road that would pass his house. If he didn't want to go with her, he better say so fast.

He did want to go to dinner with her. Very badly, but also...very close to home. "Where are we going to go?" he asked. "Somewhere in town, or are you talking a half-hour drive to get a hamburger we could get here?"

She looked at him for so long, he feared she might drive right off the road. Not that it would matter if she did. There were only fields bordering this road, and only the Johnson brothers used it.

"Here," she said. "I'm feeling like pizza. Have you been to Woodfired?"

"Many times," he said, his mouth watering and not just for pizza. He'd kissed her last week, and he really wanted to do it again. "You?"

"Many times," she repeated with a smile. "Let me guess."

She glanced at him as she drove right on past his house. "You're a traditionalist. You get meat and veggies and marinara sauce."

He chuckled, unsure if he should be pleased she knew that about him or offended that she thought he couldn't take risks. "I can neither confirm nor deny that."

"Confirmed then." She laughed, and Brian would never categorize that sound as a giggle. Everything about Seren was a step above girly, and while she was lithe and tall, she carried a *don't-mess-with-me* vibe with her that made Brian want to mess with her.

"So you probably get something like goat cheese and honey," he said. "Or even worse, five-cheese with red pepper flakes."

"Ew, no," she said as she left the ranch behind. "I don't like spicy food. Remember when you took me to that Tex-Mex place? Where was that?"

"Temple," he said, because he remembered everywhere they'd been. He'd had plenty of time on the drive home from their date to catalog it all.

"That's right," she said. "Their food was too spicy."

"But I'm right about the cheese, aren't I?"

"I guess you'll find out when we get there and I order." She gave him a fun, flirty smile he'd seen before. She was the same Seren he'd started to fall for last autumn, and he hoped that this time would be the time a relationship stuck with them.

"I just need to ask something," he said. He wasn't going to

go through with another trip to town, only to have her slip out of his life again.

"All right."

"Is this...is this what you want?"

"Is what what I want?"

"To go to dinner with me. In town. Where anyone can see us."

"Yes," she said, and just like that, the wounds that had been festering in Brian's soul healed.

"All right, then," he said.

"That's what you want, right?" she asked, glancing at him. "To go out in public."

"Yes," he said. "I want everyone to know I'm with you. You're with me, so everyone else better look the other way."

She looked at him, alarm in her eyes. She burst out laughing, and while Brian liked it, he wasn't sure what he'd said that was quite so funny.

She realized he wasn't joining in, and she sobered quickly. "You just don't get it," she said, and she didn't sound entirely happy. She hadn't turned the car around yet either.

"Then tell me," he said.

"I've been out with two guys, Brian. Two. In my whole life." She looked at him, her big, brown eyes wide and begging him to understand. "I don't know what I'm doing, and I'm obviously really bad at this dating thing."

"Actually, Seren," he said, reaching over and taking one of her hands off the wheel. He kneaded the tension out of it, trying to find the right words. "You're really good at the dating thing. We haven't ever had a bad one, have we?"

"I suppose not," she said, and he felt her relax a little bit.

"Did you talk to Sorrell about your vow?"

"Yes," she said. "She likes this cowboy, and I told her to ask him out instead of waiting for him to ask her." She glanced at him. "That's why I stopped tonight. I didn't want to wait for you to ask me again, because I don't think you would've."

"I was thinking about it," he said. "I told my brother about you."

"Tom? What did he have to say?"

"He said to follow my gut."

Seren just looked at him, and he smiled at her. "But you asked me, so I didn't have to, though I am pretty hungry for some real food, so maybe I am following my gut."

"I've seen how to get on your good side now," she said. "And I have forty-eight desserts I can get Kelly to make for me to win you over."

He wanted to tell her she'd already won him over, but his heart beat a little strangely, telling him that while he'd started to heal from her rejections, he still wasn't quite whole.

She pulled into Woodfired, and on a weekday, the parking lot wasn't overly full. They got a table immediately, one of the chest-high ones where he felt like he was on display for everyone to see.

He opened the menu, but he already knew what he wanted. "What are you going to get?"

"Nice try," Seren said, teasing him.

When their waiter came over, he ordered the Red Wonder, which was red sauce, red onions, black olives, and all kinds of red meats. Beef, bacon, sausage, and pepperoni.

"I'll take the White Outback," Seren said, handing over her menu. "With a side of garlic cheese bread."

"Two or four?"

She glanced at Brian, who shook his head. He'd gotten that garlic cheese bread before, and it had given him terrible heartburn. It was a shame, really, because he did love garlic.

"Two," Seren said.

"You got it." The waitress smiled at them and walked away.

"The White Outback?" Brian couldn't stop grinning. "It's so you." Alfredo sauce, spinach, ham, loads of cheese, and a couple of eggs cracked around the pizza and baked into it.

"Have you had it?"

"No, ma'am, I have not."

"It's delicious," she said. "It's almost like a breakfast pizza with the eggs."

"I'll have a piece," he said, looking at her. He couldn't believe he was here with her, at Woodfired, where he looked over to the next table and saw a couple he'd seen at church before. Seren followed his gaze, and she gave a little finger wave to the woman whose name Brian couldn't remember.

Seren met his eyes again, and he wanted to erase the trepidation he saw there. He'd told her stories from his childhood when they'd dated before, and she'd seemed to like them.

"Once, when Tom and I went to the carnival on the beach," he said, watching Seren perk right up. His mind raced ahead, thinking of finishing the story, trying her pizza, and then kissing her goodnight. He thought that might be a stretch for tonight, but Brian couldn't help the fantasy. After he finished the story about how he and Tom had spent an hour digging through the sand for a token, only to learn they'd all been found, he leaned toward her.

"Tell me something about your childhood, Seren," he said, smiling warmly at her. He noticed her flinch, and she took the chance to lean away from the table as their pizza arrived. With everything situated, and as she spread a napkin over her lap, he just looked at her until she met his eye. He raised his eyebrows and watched her swallow.

He waited.

CHAPTER 8

S eren didn't have any great stories the way Brian did. Any she did have, she'd told him already, last fall when they'd been seeing each other on the sly.

She picked up a slice of pizza and took a bite, watching him. "Nothing special," she said after she'd swallowed. "I've already told you about the horse that threw me, remember?" She smiled as he did, and something formed between them that Seren really liked. She couldn't name it, because she wasn't good at emotional or relationship things. Something definitely drew her to him though, and he seemed to like her.

"Right," he said. "Because of the blacksmith hammer."

"I broke two ribs." She stretched slightly on her left side. "Sometimes they still bother me." She watched him finish his first slice of pizza, wondering if what she'd shared with him would be enough.

"I bet," he said. "I had bruised ribs once after I'd ridden this mechanical bull—don't laugh." His grin could've lit a whole city, and Seren basked in the glow of it. "In Seattle, a mechanical bull was a real thing." He chuckled and shook his head. "Tom rode it, though. He was always better at balance than I was."

"Sarena's definitely the clumsiest in our family," Seren said.

"What are you?" he asked, reaching for another piece of pizza.

"What am I what?" She nudged her tray toward him. "Do you want to try mine?"

"Yes, I do." He moved to take the next piece in her pie and held it in front of him, sniffing like he was Queen.

"Okay," she said, shaking her head. "It's good. Just put it in your mouth."

He took a bite, and she knew the moment he appreciated the flavors of garlic, cream parmesan, spinach, and ham. "Mm," he said.

"See? And you barely got any egg," she said. She reached for his pizza. "Can I?"

"Please." He pushed his silver platter a little closer to her too. She took a slice of pizza, eyeing all those meats like they'd clog her arteries. With the amount she hiked, they probably wouldn't, but she still wasn't sure. She took a bite, and she shouldn't have doubted the chefs at Woodfired.

The marinara sauce had a bright, tangy flavor, and the red onion cut through some of the fattier meats. She chewed and swallowed, nodding. "That's really good too."

"What are you the most at in your family?" he asked. "The smartest, the best cook, that kind of thing."

"Definitely not the cooking," she said. "That would be Sorrell. Uh, let's see. Sarena's good with numbers and details, so that's not me." She shrugged. "If you asked them, they'd say I'm the bluntest. I just say things how they are." She smiled like that was a good quality to have, but she wasn't sure it was.

Brian reached across the table and took her hand in his. "That you do, Seren."

"Do you hate that?"

"Hate it?" He shook his head. "Nah, it's fine. Doesn't bother me."

"I'm the least emotional," she added, not sure why she was still talking. Her mood fell a bit and she squeezed his hand. "I'm not really like other women."

"That doesn't bother me either."

Seren nodded, but she wasn't so sure. The first man she'd been out with had called her a robot, and Seren had simply taken it. "I'm really good at compartmentalizing. That's why I don't get super emotional about things too often."

"What does it take for you to get super emotional?" he asked, picking off a piece of pepperoni with his free hand. He glanced up at her, his eyes barely visible beneath the brim of that cowboy hat she liked so much.

"I don't know," she said.

"What about when your dad died?"

Seren remembered the day clearly, and all the days afterward. She zeroed in on each moment of time, one right after the other, and then zipped back to the table in the restaurant with Brian. "I didn't cry," she said. "There was so much to do, and Sorrell was a mess. Sarena was too, just in a different way."

She looked at Brian, feeling broken inside. Who didn't cry when their father died? "I stuffed everything away, and I got the job done. I'm really good at that."

He nodded and reached for his drink.

Seren picked up a piece of garlic cheese toast and cocked her head. "I'm sad about my parents, but it's...weird. It's like something that comes and goes, and not something I carry around all the time."

"Do you miss them?"

"Every day," she said simply. She wasn't a monster. She just didn't weep all the time. She didn't worry about things she couldn't control, and for maybe the first time, she didn't think she was the worst person on the planet because she didn't cry every time something was hard.

"Ready?" he asked when she finished her garlic cheese bread.

"Yes." She boxed up her leftovers, because they'd be great to take to work, and they went out to her car. The drive back to Chestnut Ranch happened seemingly in the blink of an eye, and before Seren knew it, she was facing Brian's front porch.

She glanced to the cabin next door, and back down the road the way she'd come.

"Are you going to take the job here?" Brian asked.

She seized onto the topic, because she needed something to propel her up to his porch. "What do you think?"

"I think you could quote them a lot and they'd pay it," he said, taking slow steps down the sidewalk toward where he'd left his guitar leaning against the railing.

Seren did need the money for the air conditioner, even if

all she did was use it to pay Darren back later on. "Yeah," she said. "I'll take it."

"Great," he said. "I'm the project manager over the remodel, and I'll send you the timeline and everything. Painting is a while off." He looked up into the dusky sky. "Thanks for going to dinner with me, Seren." He took her effortlessly into his arms, and Seren breathed in the musky, male scent of his shirt, which also held a bit of marinara from the pizza parlor.

"It was fun," she said, and she meant it.

"I'll call you later, okay?" He pulled back and raised his eyebrows.

She nodded, not allowing herself to look at his lips, and turned back to her car. A sigh moved through her whole body, and she rode the adrenaline high of a successful date with Brian all the way back to the ranch.

* * *

SEREN WOKE WHEN A ROUGH, canine tongue licked her cheek. "No, Koda," she said, moaning as she pushed the golden retriever away and rolled over. He settled right against her back, and she felt bad she'd shunned him.

She reached over and stroked him, unsurprised the dog rolled over on his back so she'd rub his belly. "You're a softie," she said to him, waking more fully now. She kept her eyes closed though, her thoughts centering on Brian. She'd been amazingly busy at work the past few days, and he'd had a dog crisis at Chestnut Ranch, so they hadn't seen each other again.

Sarena had been dealing with her own mess of snakes here at Fox Hollow, as some of the cattle had come down with some sort of sickness that she hadn't been able to diagnose yet. She'd been complaining about how she didn't have a vet on-staff, and that she didn't even have enough help on the ranch.

Because of that, Seren had managed to avoid another conversation about Brian with her oldest sister. Sorrell had adapted to the newer kitchen appliances here just fine, and Seren was very grateful for the air conditioning that kept her cool enough to sleep at night.

When she arrived in full consciousness, she realized by tomorrow night, she'd be sleeping at the homestead. The air conditioner repairmen were supposed to be coming today and tomorrow.

That gave her enough gumption to get out of bed and start getting ready for work. She was halfway to Enchantment Rock when her phone zinged at her. She glanced at where it rested in the cup holder and saw Brian's name on the screen.

Her pulse jumped, but she kept both hands on the wheel. She eventually made it to the employee parking lot at Enchantment Rock State Park, and since she wasn't late that morning, she took a moment to read his text.

What time are you done tonight? Barring anything major going wrong at the ranch, I'd love to go to dinner with you.

A warm feeling spread through Seren's body, making her extremities tingle. "I should be off by six," she dictated as she typed. She sent the message and got out of the car. She'd just signed in for the day when she got another message.

Great, Brian had said. *Six-thirty then?*

Sure, she said, pocketing her phone as her supervisor came out of her office. "Morning, Miranda."

"Oh, good, Seren." The older woman smiled at Seren, and Seren could see her future right in front of her. Miranda had dark hair too, though hers was much shorter than Seren's and cut into a fashionable bob. She had dark eyes and plenty of wrinkles around her eyes. Her skin seemed stained from many years of leading groups up to the rock and back down. "Just the woman I wanted to see."

"What's up?"

"I just got a booking for a private stargazer tonight, and I need you to do it."

Seren's date with Brian disappeared into a hazy dot on the horizon. She wanted to protest, because she literally never said no to a stargazer. Watching the sun set from the top of Enchantment Rock was the most beautiful sight in the world, and Seren felt closer to herself, and to God, every time she led a group up in the near-darkness.

"I don't think I can tonight," she said, frowning.

"You were requested," Miranda said, a twinkling smile on her face.

Surprise shot through Seren. "By who?"

"They wanted it to be a surprise." Miranda took a step around the sign-in desk and said, "Belinda, wait up a minute, would you? I need to talk to you about the map display." With that, Miranda was gone, hustling off to catch up to the retail manager over the gift shop and ranger's desk in the visitor's center.

She pulled out her phone to text Brian the bad news, her heart falling down somewhere around her toes.

Hey, sorry—

"Seren, your group is five minutes from leaving," someone said, and she looked up, startled. Sure enough, the time had slipped away from her, and she needed to get outside to the meeting area.

She quickly grabbed her pack and made sure the water pouch was full. She always kept her pack stocked and ready, so she didn't have to arrive at work too much earlier than when her first tour started. She plucked her hat from the hook beside her pack and stepped out the back door she'd entered through.

Down the sidewalk and around the building, a group of about twenty-five people milled around, and Seren put her guide-smile on her face. "Good morning, everyone," she called as she approached. "This will be the nine a.m. guided hike to the top of the rock. Are you all in the right place?"

A couple of the nearest people gave their assent, but that wasn't good enough for Seren. "Oh, come on," she said, her smile feeling particularly plastic today. "I think my feeble grandmother could be louder than that." She laughed lightly and adjusted the straps on her backpack. "I said, this is the nine a.m. guided hike to the top of the rock. Who's excited?"

That got the tourists whooping, and she laughed with a couple of them. "All right. Let's get going, because there is so much to see out here."

Seren led two groups up the rock and back down before she stepped back into the blessedly air-conditioned building for lunch. She hadn't had a spare moment to communicate with Brian, and he hadn't cancelled yet either. She'd been hoping he would, because then she wouldn't have to.

"Hey," she said to Meg as she sat at the table with her.

"No lunch today?"

"Oh, right. Lunch." Distracted, Seren got up and managed to get her lunch out of the freezer. She kept several microwavable meals here in the break room for days when she didn't have any leftovers to bring—or when she was late. Sorrell had endured a late meeting at the community center the previous night, and she'd eaten leftovers by herself as Darren and Sarena had been out on the ranch late again.

With her steaming chicken pot pie in front of her, she rejoined Meg at the table.

"Rough morning?" her friend asked.

"What? No, it was great." She looked up from her phone. "I just...I had a date with this guy tonight, and I just found out I have to do a private stargazer. I don't want to tell him I have to cancel."

"Okay, so let's pause." Meg held up both hands, and she could be dramatic. Seren loved her anyway, because so much of what Seren felt like she was missing, she could find in Meg. "You have a date tonight? With a man? And I'm just hearing about it?"

Seren ducked her head and smiled at the chicken pot pie crust. "He just asked this morning."

"So it's not something you've had set up for a while."

"Mm, nope." She broke into her pie and let the steam escape. "But we sort of went to dinner the other night too, and I haven't seen him since. So it's kind of a big deal."

"Uh, yeah," Meg said, her eyes widening. "You going on a *first* date is a big deal."

Seren looked down the table, but the nearest person was Flo, and she wore hearing aids in both ears. Even if she had heard, Seren wouldn't care. "Can you keep your voice down?" Something pinched behind her lungs, though Meg wasn't saying anything untrue.

"Sorry." Meg patted her arm. "Really. I am. So who is this guy?"

"Just a guy," Seren said, though that wasn't true at all. Not even a little bit true. Brian Gray was much more than "a guy," even if Seren hadn't admitted it to herself yet.

"Okay, let's table that for a minute and come back to it. Just tell him you're sorry, and ask him to dinner tomorrow."

Seren put a bite of piping hot pot pie in her mouth and picked up her phone. Sorrell had texted about having a cele-bratory bash at the farmhouse tomorrow night, *complete with air conditioning!* she'd said, and an idea began to form in her mind.

Can I invite someone? she asked her sister.

Brian? Sorrell sent back

Yes.

Meg watched the conversation over Seren's forearm, nudging her with her shoulder. "Good one. Yes, invite him back to the house for a celebratory dinner. Good move."

"Is it?" Seren asked, looking at her.

"Of course it is," Meg said. "It's personal. It involves family. You're not hiding him. That kind of thing."

Hiding him. Seren hadn't thought keeping things secret

with him was that big of a deal, but maybe it was. Meg had definitely been out with way more people than Seren had, so she would know.

"Brian who?" Meg asked.

"Gray," Seren said. "He works at Chestnut Ranch."

"Oooh, a cowboy." Meg made a smacking noise with her lips. "I like cowboys."

Seren giggled as Sorrell confirmed that she could invite Brian, and she sent him a quick message too. *Hey, I just found out I have to work the night hike tonight, so I can't have dinner. But what about you coming to the farmhouse tomorrow for dinner? Sorrell's making a big meal to celebrate our new air conditioner.*

Before she could second-guess herself or even check the spelling of the text, she sent it. Brian worked on the ranch all the time, and she knew he didn't check his phone often. She couldn't either, and they'd learned to text before work, during lunch, or after work, sometimes late into the night depending on what they'd both been dealing with.

She'd just set her phone on the table when it rang.

"Oh, it's Brian," Meg said, her tone full of glee.

Seren stood and swept the phone off the table at the same time, her pulse lodging somewhere in the back of her throat. "Hey," she answered as she walked away from her best friend.

"Hey," Brian said, and his voice sent shivers through her muscles. "So I've been outside in the hot sun all morning. I've broken up two dog fights already, so my brain might be addled, but I swear your text said to come to dinner at the farmhouse tomorrow night..." His tone held a note of teasing, though he was probably serious in asking. She'd never let him come to the farmhouse before, and Seren realized what a big step this was for them. For her, really.

She ducked out the back door and pressed her back into the hot brick of the building. A giggle came out of her mouth. "That's what it said all right."

"Seren," he said, dead serious now. A lengthy pause followed. "Really?"

"Yes, really," Seren said, removing the flirtation from her voice too. "My sisters will be there, and Sarena is so nosy you'll be sorry you've been wanting to come pick me up from the farmhouse."

"I don't think so," he said, no trace of sarcasm in any of the words. "What time?"

"Six-thirty," she said. "If you can."

He sighed, and she knew the feeling of exhaustion and being out of control. "Things are hectic right now, but I'll do my best. I can check in with you throughout the day?"

"Of course," she said. "Just like me having to work tonight."

"Yeah, tell me about that," he said.

"Oh, someone called and scheduled a private stargazer, and they specifically requested me." She shook her head and went back inside, because there was no sense standing out in the heat if she didn't have to. "My boss didn't really give me a choice."

"Too bad," he said as a dog started barking on his end of the line. Then another. "Listen, I have to go." She could barely hear him as a third dog—this one obviously much closer than the other two—joined the canine conversation.

"Talk to you later," she practically yelled. She ended the call and looked up. Everyone in the break room was staring at her. Meg burst out laughing, and that got everyone else chuckling too, Seren included.

"Stop it," she said to Meg, but the two of them just started laughing again.

"So," Meg said when she'd calmed. "Tomorrow night?"

"It's a go," Seren said, wolfing down a few bites of her pot pie so she could get to the bathroom and then out to greet her next group. "I'll keep you posted."

She put on a brave face and kept her shoulders straight as she strode away, but inside, she was a jiggly jumble of goo. She hoped inviting Brian to the farmhouse for dinner with her sisters wasn't a mistake.

Sarena really could be nosy and overbearing.

Sorrell could feel betrayed, though she'd said Seren should date.

It was really the fear of the unknown that had Seren's stomach in a knot, and no matter how she tried to work it out, it just grew tighter and tighter.

CHAPTER 9

Brian's nerves fired a shot of adrenaline through him every few seconds. He gripped the wheel and told himself to just keep driving. "She's going to be excited," he told himself, and he hoped he was right.

Seren had called him on her dinner break, and she'd sounded upset. Not upset in an emotional kind of way but upset in an angry way. She was not happy she had to stay for the private stargazing hike.

He hoped she'd be excited when he arrived, the only person booked for that hike. He had specifically requested her, and he had dinner in the back seat. That should win her over for sure.

Brian hadn't meant to test her, but he'd wanted to know what she'd do when she couldn't get together with him. Would she insist she couldn't work? Would she be upset when she had to cancel?

She'd reacted the way he'd hoped she would, though he

hated that he'd staged the stargazer hike to judge if he should really take another step with her.

Armed with hope that they could have a meaningful future together, he kept the truck going toward Enchantment Rock.

He pulled through the gate and followed the signs. Miranda had told him Seren would meet him out front, as the rest of the visitor's center was closed. Sure enough, he saw her sitting on the bench, a pack at her feet and her eyes on her phone, the moment he came around the bend in the road.

His pulse pounded in his ears, and when she looked up at the sound of his truck, he couldn't help but smile.

She got to her feet but didn't move, and Brian was able to pull to the curb, stop, and get out before anything even registered on her face. "You're the private stargazer," she said, and it wasn't a question.

"Yep." His heart continued to boom in his chest as he opened the back door and got out their dinner. He rounded the front of the truck with the covered tray, adding, "We don't have to hike up to the rock. I know you've led four groups today."

She looked at the industrial sized tray, swallowed, and looked back at him. "What is that? It smells amazing."

"Doesn't it?" He gestured for her to sit again. "Wait. Is there a picnic table somewhere? Or can we go inside?" It wasn't exactly cool outdoors right now.

"Let's go inside," she said. "I have a key to the back door." She gave him a smile that made him hope he could kiss her later, and led the way around the small visitor's center. It was much cooler inside, and he set the tray on a long table.

He took off the lid and said, "It's brisket and mashed potatoes." He looked from the food to her face. Her eyes had widened, and she stared at their dinner. "From Fat Joe's."

Slowly, her gaze met his. "I love Fat Joe's."

"I know," he said, smiling. "That's why I brought it."

Her face held wonder, but it crumpled in the next moment, and she rushed at him. He managed to catch her in his arms and breathe her in.

"Thank you," she said, plenty of emotion in her voice then. She backed up and looked at the food again. "I had a bag of chips from the vending machine and an old granola bar from my pack for dinner."

Brian chuckled, his heart throbbing for her. "Well, now you get brisket and barbecue sauce."

They settled down to eat, and Brian couldn't help watching her covertly. She talked about her day, and then said, "We should go hiking together sometime. I can show you some amazing things not everyone knows about."

"Yeah, sure," he said. "I'll go hiking with you, if you'll go horseback riding with me." He quirked his eyebrows at her, thinking that she'd say no. She didn't seem to be the Adams sister that liked doing much on a ranch.

"I think I can do that," she said, nudging him with her shoulder. "I can't wait to get back to the house and see how the air conditioner is working."

"I can't believe the air conditioner went out," he said. "Doesn't God know there's a heat wave in Texas?"

She laughed and shook her head. "He knows, he just thought he'd throw a wrench at me and Sorrell." She gave him a smile that told him she didn't really believe that. "Darren paid for the air conditioner," she said. "We're just going to pay him back over time."

Brian's throat narrowed, but he managed to nod. "Smart." He wondered if she'd say anything more about why Darren had the money to pay for a new air conditioner, but she didn't.

She finished eating, and when their eyes met again, she leaned toward him. That was all the encouragement he needed, and he quickly closed the distance between them to kiss her.

A sigh moved through his whole soul, and Brian felt like kissing Seren was equivalent to the stars aligning.

The following afternoon, Brian checked the time on his phone, rationalizing that it wouldn't take long at Seth's to look at the man's computer. He'd called twenty minutes ago, complaining that he couldn't get it to connect to the printer, and he wanted Brian to come look at it.

Out of everyone on the ranch, only Seth knew about Brian's technological past. Only Seth knew how much money Brian had in his bank account, and only Seth could get Brian to come over to look at his system when he should be getting in the shower so he wasn't late for his date at the ranch next door.

Darren also knew about Brian's money, but he only

worked at Chestnut part-time now. To Brian's knowledge, neither of them had ever told anyone else about Brian's past. He'd said a few things here and there to the other cowboys, but for the most part, Brian had left Seattle for a reason, and he saw no point in telling everyone about it.

He pulled into the long driveway at the manor house next-door to the ranch, where Queen jumped from the back of the truck before he'd even gotten out of the cab. She loved Seth and Jenna, and she seemed to know this was where they lived.

"You're supposed to wait for me," he told her as he climbed the front steps behind her. She already had two paws up on the final step that led into the house, and she looked up at the door, waiting for him to open it.

He rang the doorbell instead, and told her to sit. She did, and Brian bent down to pat her.

Seth opened the door and said, "Hey," before the German shepherd rushed him. "Oh, hello to you too, Queen." He laughed and scratched behind Queen's ears. "She's really great, Brian."

"I think she causes all the fights in the yard," he said, stepping into the house and closing the door behind him.

"The others will settle down once they realize she's the alpha." He went past the piano studio on the left and the office on the right. Brian followed him into the kitchen and living area, where Seth indicated the computer sitting benignly on a built-in desk.

"She's got intense energy," Brian said. "They should calm down though."

"It's all Benz anyway," Seth said. "I'm working with him."

"Yeah," Brian said, eying the computer. "Sit, Queen." The dog did as he said, and he beamed at her.

"She's so great," Seth said. "You're lucky you got one like her as an adult."

Brian met his friend's eye. "She's an ex-police dog," he said. "One that actually failed their program. She better know how to sit when I say."

"Is that right?" Seth crouched down in front of her and stroked both hands down the sides of her face. Queen seemed to melt right into his touch, as the man had a real knack for dogs. They loved him, and he loved them, and it was almost like he could hear what they were thinking. "You're definitely a police dog. Where'd you get her?"

"Dallas," Brian said.

"Is that why you went down there?" Seth straightened. "I guess I just didn't put two and two together."

"She's four years old," Brian said. "She couldn't locate fast enough, and they were selling her."

"How much?" Seth asked. "If you don't mind me asking."

Brian's rule had just come into play. If no one asked, he didn't tell. Seth had asked.

"Six thousand," he said, looking away. "She's a great dog, and exactly what I wanted."

"You don't have to justify anything to me," Seth said. "I just wish you'd let me pay you."

"I don't need the money."

"I know," he said. "But neither do I."

Their eyes met, and Brian broke first, as usual. He ducked

his head as he shook it, a chuckle coming from his mouth. "I've told you what to do with my salary."

"I haven't found the right charity."

"Right," Brian said dryly. "That means you haven't looked."

"The ranch is crazy right now," Seth said.

"That it is." Brian sat at the machine, glad he'd finally told someone about Queen. "What's it doing?"

"It says it's connected to the printer, but I can't print."

Brian started clicking around, finding the utilities and permissions he needed. Sometimes he really missed being in front of a computer. Then he'd remember the big blanket of sky that had stretched over his head last night as he'd driven home after his date with Seren. He didn't stay up to actually see the stars, but he'd seen them before here in the Texas Hill Country. They were something to behold, and then he didn't miss his work in Seattle quite so much.

About sixty seconds later, the printer started to whir. "There you go."

"How did you do that?" Seth shook his head, a disgruntled look on his face that quickly morphed into a smile. "I feel like an idiot now."

"You just had the wrong server connected to it," he said. "I made them the same, and *voilà*. Printing." He picked up the paper and glanced at it before handing it to Seth. He didn't say anything, though he'd seen an adoption form like this before.

"Thanks," Seth said, looking at the paper too. He smiled at Brian. "What are you doing for dinner? Jenna ran something in to her brother, because he's been working so much. But she should be back soon."

"I have a date," Brian said, unable to hold the smile back once again. Even thinking about Seren brought a curve to his mouth. "Thanks, but I'm going to do that."

Seth grinned too. "Wow, you're dating?"

"Kind of," Brian said, though in his mind, he and Seren were totally dating. "I'm going over to her place tonight." He clapped Seth on the shoulder as he went past. "I need to go shower, and I can't be late. You should be good with that now."

"Thanks," Seth said again, and Brian hurried back to his cabin. Tom had often said Brian was part robot with the ease with which he worked with computers. At times, Brian felt that way too. He simply knew what to do and how computers worked. They were predictable, and ran on patterns, and he understood all of that.

What he didn't understand was whether he should shave or not. He had no idea what shirt to wear to go all the way to the farmhouse for the first time. He wasn't sure what would happen once he arrived, but he reminded himself that he knew Seren's sisters. He'd been to the farmhouse before.

There was something different about tonight, though, and he knew it. Seren knew it too, which was why she'd texted no less than ten times that day, asking him if he liked veggie pizza.

He'd called it an oxymoron. He wasn't sure why anyone would choose to put only vegetables on a pizza, but he'd told her he'd eat anything. He would, and he wouldn't care, because he'd be with Seren.

Not only that, but she'd invited him all the way to the farmhouse.

"Come on, Queen," he said to his dog, who lounged on the couch. "Let's go see Koda." Queen got along great with Darren's dog, and her ears perked up at his name.

Brian got her in the back of the truck and situated himself behind the wheel. Fox Hollow wasn't that far away—only about fifteen minutes—and he glanced at the dashboard clock. "Is that really the time?"

He only had seven minutes before he was supposed to arrive for dinner. He'd been known to go over the speed limit in a real emergency, and this definitely felt like a real emergency.

By the time he trucked down the lane—all the way down the lane—to Seren's front door, he was five minutes late. He got out and took a deep breath, hoping this night was the first of many great experiences with Seren. It was either that, or things would be so bad he'd have to break up with her again.

He went up the steps and rang the doorbell, his breath hitching in his chest. Finally, he could hear footsteps approaching on the other side of the door, and it swung open a moment later.

Seren stood there, and she'd stolen his breath, his ability to stand up straight and tall, and every ounce of his attention. She wore a pair of white shorts that went mid-way down her thigh and a navy blue tank top with tiny white dots on it.

He couldn't wait to kiss her again, and he couldn't wait to step inside this house. It felt like a leap, and he found he really wanted to take it—if only Seren would invite him to come in.

CHAPTER 10

S eren drank in the form of Brian Gray standing on the porch. His dog came forward as if she sensed a kindred spirit inside Seren's body, and she bent down to say hello. "Oh, you're such a good girl, Queen," she said, basking in the warm energy of the German shepherd.

"We're not cooling the whole farm," Sorrell called, and Seren straightened and gestured for Brian to come in. Her nerves knocked through her body, because this was the first time he'd been to the farmhouse just to see her. He was the first man she'd introduced to her sisters as her boyfriend in a decade.

He pressed in close to her, his left hand grazing her hip as he went by. "Hey, Seren," he said, his voice so deep it almost sounded muted. "You look nice tonight."

She better, because she'd spent forty minutes with the flat-iron, heating out every crinkle in her hair. She'd put on lip gloss and mascara at Sorrell's insistence, because her sister claimed that she'd feel better if she looked her best.

Seren could admit—grudgingly—that she did feel like a million bucks, especially when Brian paused at the edge of the foyer and waited for her to close the door and come to his side. "Thanks," she said. "You look great too."

He wore jeans and his cowboy boots, though probably not the ones he wore around the ranch. These seemed dust-free and scuff-free, so he probably only wore them to movie theaters and church. His blue and white plaid shirt brought out the azure in his eyes, the glinting gold among the darker brown hair in his beard, and his sideburns.

He took her hand and squeezed, and Seren tried to squeeze a smile onto her face too. It felt a little pinched, and her heartbeat sounded like a drum in her own ears. "Ready for this?"

"I know your sisters," he said.

"Yeah." It was one of the arguments he'd given her before, when he'd wanted to come to the front door to pick her up for dinner and a movie. Instead, she'd made him meet her in the parking lot at Enchantment Rock or down the road a bit.

Her stomach flipped, and not in a good way. "Better get this over with." She got herself moving down the hall and into the expansive living room. Beyond that sat the dining table, with eight chairs tonight, properly set for a real meal. Most of the time, she and Sorrell sat at the bar, but Sorrell had that lined with food tonight.

"The air conditioner is working great," Brian commented as everyone in the kitchen turned toward their arrival.

Seren's first instinct was to run away. Veer left and past the stairs that went down into the basement and head toward the bedrooms beyond this main living area. "Yeah," she said, her voice a bit numb. "It works great."

"Have you been sleeping at Sarena's?"

"Yes," she said, glancing at him. He didn't seem to notice the other three cowboys in the house, or her two sisters. "It's our first night back. I'm excited to sleep in my own bed."

"I bet you are." He stepped in front of her, making her blink as he blocked her view of the kitchen. "Hey." He reached up and ran his fingers down the side of her face, sending fireworks through her skin and into her mouth. "Are you okay?"

"Nervous," she murmured.

"I know all of these people," he said.

"Yeah." But that wasn't why *she* was nervous. *She* was nervous because she didn't know how to be the female half of a couple. She didn't know how to call him her boyfriend. With a sudden realization, she thought maybe she wouldn't have to.

He already knows all these people.

No introductions necessary, right?

As soon as Brian left, though, Seren would have to endure dozens of questions from her sisters. There was no escaping that.

He moved back to her side, and Seren led him past the couches and armchairs and into the kitchen. She had no idea what to say.

"Hey, Brian," Darren said, stepping away from the vegetable tray and crackers and dip to shake his friend's hand. "How are you?"

"Good," Brian said with a smile. "Sorrell, all of this looks amazing."

Seren blinked, trying to remember what her sister had made for dinner. She had all the syrups out on the end of the counter for flavored sodas or coffee. A big bowl of salad. Two pizzas, already cut. Appetizers.

"Thanks, Brian," she said. "I think we're all here, and this last pizza only has a couple of minutes, so let's say grace, and it might be done." She looked at Sarena, who was staring at Seren. A couple of seconds passed, where Seren acted like she'd never seen a pizza before, and Sarena kept staring at the side of her face.

"Sarena?" Sorrell asked.

"Right," her oldest sister said, finally tearing her eyes from Seren. "I'll say grace, and then we'll eat."

"I thought you said you had something you wanted to tell everyone," Sorrell said. "The last pizza has a couple more minutes."

Seren sneaked a peek at Sarena, who shook herself and sighed. "Oh, right. Yes. I did have something I wanted to say." She swallowed and reached for Darren, who moved away from Brian and Seren to join his wife's side.

"It's good news, so you can stop worrying, Sorrell," she said with a smile. She gazed at Darren for a moment, and Seren knew exactly what was going to come out of her mouth. Sorrell did too, because she sucked in a breath.

"She's going to scream," Seren whispered, bracing herself.

Serena faced the group. "Things around the ranch might change a little bit." She looked at Theo and Stephen, the two full-time cowboys that worked at Fox Hollow with Sarena. "Because Darren and I are going to have a baby."

Seren pointed at Sorrell, who shrieked just as Seren had predicted she would. Sorrell was always the most dramatic of the sisters, and Seren let her weep and hug Sarena first. Happiness turned into joy as she thought about being an aunt to Sarena's children.

"Congratulations," she said, stepping over to Sarena and Darren and hugging them both at the same time. "How exciting."

They both possessed a glow she couldn't believe she'd missed over the past few evenings while she'd been in their home. She hadn't noticed Sarena being sick, but she also didn't monitor when her sister went to work in the morning or what she did all day.

"Thank you, Seren," Sarena whispered. When all the congratulations had gone around, she said, "I might look into hiring some more help around here, but we're still a few months away, so we'll see."

"When is the baby due?" Theo asked, glancing from Sorrell to Sarena.

"November," Sarena said.

"Birthing season." Theo's expression darkened.

"I'm not going to leave you high and dry," Sarena said. "But yes, there will be a lot of birthing on the ranch in November."

"Okay," Darren said, shaking his head. "That was a terrible joke."

Stephen laughed, and even Seren managed to crack a smile.

The timer on the oven went off, and Sorrell flew into gear, getting it out and placing it in the empty spot on the counter. She explained the different pizzas, Stephen said grace, and it was time to eat.

The seven of them filled their plates and took spots at the table, and Seren started to relax a little bit. Brian did know the other cowboys there, and he easily slipped into talking to Darren about things happening at Chestnut, the other friends they had, and his new dog.

Seren listened to their conversation, but she also kept an ear on the one happening with Theo, Stephen, Sarena, and Sorrell as they talked about life at Fox Hollow Ranch, how it would change, how it wouldn't, and then how the construction on the new hay loft was coming along.

Seren hadn't even been aware of construction on a new hay loft, and she felt adrift. Stuck between two conversations, neither of which she could really participate in.

"So," Darren said. "How long have you and Seren been going out?"

She tensed, immediately withdrawing her attention from the other conversation at the table to focus on Brian's answer.

"Not long," he said, glancing at her. "Less than a week."

She frowned, because that wasn't true. Or was it? She had no idea how relationships worked.

Darren nodded like it was perfectly normal for Brian to be at this family dinner when their relationship was less than a week old. "How's the family in Seattle?"

"Just Tom's in Seattle," Brian said, and at least Seren knew he was talking about his brother.

"I know you've been seeing him for more than a week," Sarena said, practically leaning over the table to say it soft enough not to disturb the other conversations. But without her contributing to the talk about the ranch, the others had fallen silent. So they all heard her too.

Seren glanced at Sorrell and Theo, then back to Sarena. "Not officially," she said.

"Was it him last year?" Sarena asked.

Seren wanted to kick her under the table. She didn't answer, and instead turned back to Darren and Brian, who were talking about some computerized software that would make ranching easier.

"I keep telling Sarena about it," Darren said, glancing at his wife. "She's not convinced."

"It would be great," Brian said, looking at her with a new light in his eye Seren had never seen before. "It tracks everything, Sarena. Water percentages, feed levels, birthing cycles." He was so animated as he spoke about it, that Seren felt like she was sitting beside a man she'd never met before.

He glanced at her and sat back in his seat. "I love computers and stuff like that."

"I can see that," Seren said.

"It makes sense," Darren said.

"What does?" Seren asked.

"Oh, you haven't told her." Darren looked at Sarena and then Brian. "And now I just told her. Shoot. I'm sorry, Brian."

"Told me what?" Seren asked.

"Yeah," Sarena said. "Told her what?"

Brian took another bite of his pizza, but it sure seemed like chewing it was hard for him. He put the other half down, wiped his mouth with a napkin, and looked between the two sisters, finally letting his gaze land on Seren. "I worked in the tech industry in Seattle before I came here."

"I did know that." She narrowed her eyes. "There has to be more."

"Not much," Brian said with a shrug, but Seren hadn't been born yesterday. There was definitely more. A lot more. He just didn't want to say.

"Peach pie," Sorrell sang out, and that saved him from having to say. Seren met his eye, and they both knew it. Thankfully, her nosy sister didn't press him to keep talking, though Seren could tell she wanted to.

Darren put his hand on her forearm and leaned close to her, saying something. She nodded and stood up. "I'll get the whipped cream, Sorrell." She took her plate into the kitchen and opened the fridge.

Seren looked down at her half-eaten food, wondering why she felt like such a stranger among the people she knew and loved best.

People got up and moved around her, taking plates into the kitchen, pouring coffee, and collecting plates of peach pie with plenty of whipped cream.

"Are you finished?" Brian asked, and she looked up to find him standing next to her.

"Yes."

He took her plate and went a couple of steps before turning back. "Do you want pie?"

She nodded and stood up too, though she had nowhere to

go. She just didn't want to be the only one still at the table, as Stephen, Theo, Sarena, and Darren had taken their coffee and dessert into the living room.

Only Sorrell remained in the kitchen, and she scooped pie for Brian and Seren and joined everyone else.

Brian held two plates of pie in his hands and nodded toward the back door.

Escape.

Seren didn't have to think twice. She practically ran for the door.

CHAPTER 11

Relief cascaded over Brian like a waterfall as he left the farmhouse. He couldn't close the door behind him, and Seren was already at the edge of the deck, her long legs eating up distance with every stride. He set one plate of pie down on a nearby table and returned to the door to close it.

"Curse Darren Dumond," he muttered to himself as he returned to the table to get the pie. Now he had to tell Seren about his software. His sale. His money. His escape from Seattle.

Or did he?

She obviously hadn't told him everything about herself, and he wasn't even sure he believed her for why she hadn't wanted to bring their relationship to light sooner.

So he definitely needed a lot of pie for tonight's conversation. He made it to the edge of the deck too, the backyard here completely shaded in the evening. It was still hot, but bearable. Beautiful, too.

"Seren?" he called, because he hadn't seen which way she'd gone.

Footsteps sounded to his left, and he caught sight of her coming back toward him on a dirt path. He went down the steps to the yard and then toward her. "Your pie." He held it out to her, balancing the fork with his thumb.

She said nothing as she took it, and perfect trouble sat on her face.

"What's wrong?" he asked.

"I'm just not good at this kind of stuff," she said, turning away from him.

"Eating dinner with your friends and family?"

"It's more than that, Brian."

"Is it?" He hurried to keep up with her. "What is it, then?"

"I told you I haven't been out with anyone in a long time. Years. A decade." She seemed to walk faster with every step she took.

Brian didn't even try to keep up with her. He just let her go ahead to a picnic table that sat in the middle of three big, beautiful oaks. She sat down, and Brian joined her a few seconds later.

"So you're out of practice," he said, trying to be gentle. "It was fine."

"Was it?" She swept her fork through the top peak of her whipped cream and looked at him, unrest in her eyes. "I didn't have anything to say to anyone at dinner. I don't work on a ranch. I didn't even know we were doing construction here." She shook her head and lowered her eyes again. "I don't fit."

"Yes, you do," he said. "Of course you do."

"And then, on top of all my other awkwardness, I find out you have something you haven't told me from Seattle, and I've got my sister in my face saying she doesn't believe how long we've been going out." She met his eyes again, and Brian thought that was fairly positive. "So I'm not sure what your version of *fine* is, but that wasn't it for me."

"I didn't know what to say about how long we'd been going out," he admitted. "Seems to me that it's been less than a week. Last fall and winter doesn't count. We broke up. Even last week doesn't count. We broke up."

"So we're going with…when?"

"The night you stopped by my house and let me take you to Woodfired," he said. "In public. That was the first date."

Seren nodded. "I guess that makes sense."

"It does to me." Brian took his first bite of pie, prepared to say something else. But the cold, sweet peaches, delectable whipped cream, and flaky pie crust made a moan move through his throat instead. "Oh, my goodness," he said. "This is amazing."

"I can't cook," Seren blurted. "Just so you know. There's not going to be peach pie at our house."

Brian swallowed and looked at her. "Okay," he said. But there was clearly so much more wrong. "Keep talking, Seren."

"I told you. I don't fit. I'm not a domestic goddess like Sorrell. I don't work a ranch by myself, with a prosthetic, while I'm pregnant, like Sarena." Her chest lifted and fell as if she were having a hard time breathing. "Why do you even like me?"

Brian put down his fork, though he very much wanted to have another bite of pie. "*Because* you're not a domestic goddess like Sorrell," he said quietly. "If I liked what I saw in Sorrell, I'd have asked her out. *Because* you don't run a ranch —and I didn't even know Sarena had a prosthetic. But it doesn't matter." He reached across the table and took both of her hands in his. "I like you, Serendipity, because you're the most beautiful woman I've ever met, and you chased me down to give me your number."

He gave her a grin, actually a little surprised when the corners of her mouth curved up too. "You don't need to be anyone but yourself."

"No one's ever liked her very much," she whispered.

"Well, *I* do," Brian said. He released her hands. "I would like you to tell me the truth about why you didn't want anyone to know about us. But I still like you."

She raised her eyes to his. "I have told you the truth about that."

"Yeah," he said. "The same way I told you about my life in Seattle."

Her eyes widened, and Brian just looked steadily back at her. "There's more," she finally said.

"To both stories," he said. "And I figure, it's cool out here. There's a little breeze. We have pie and privacy." He shrugged, his next words unbelievable to him. "I'll go first if you promise to tell me the whole truth this time."

Go first.

He didn't want to go first.

He didn't want to say anything at all.

Seren said, "Okay," and Brian had no choice.

"Okay." He nodded and bought himself a little bit of time by taking another bite of pie, this one twice as big as the first. How would she react when she learned about his money? He wanted to think she wouldn't care. But he'd literally never met anyone who didn't care—unless they had a bank account with nine figures in it too. Those people didn't care. Seth Johnson didn't care.

Everyone else?

They cared.

Seren already felt inferior to her sisters. Brian didn't want her to feel inferior to him too.

"Okay," he said, his taste buds wanting more pie, but his stomach telling him to stop until the story was over. "I grew up in Seattle. I went to school there. My parents divorced, and they live in different cities now. You know all of that. I worked at a massive tech firm in Seattle—the biggest at the time. I never finished college. I'd been building apps since the age of fifteen, and my boss sent me down to Austin all the time. It's a big tech city too."

His throat protested when he tried to swallow again, but he managed to do it. "Anyway, I built several apps for my company, and they sold well. Really well. I became the lead developer by age twenty-three, and I had dozens of people older than me working on my team."

"Wow," Seren said.

"Yeah." Brian could see himself from all those years ago.

He thought he'd been happy. He really did love computers and apps and technology. "It was a...good life. Very busy. Very hectic. I thought I was happy." He blinked, trying to keep himself on this Texas farm instead of in the past. "At night, I started working on a couple of apps I was interested in doing. Not stuff for the company. In fact, services my firm had decided *not* to develop. There were three apps—a family, we call them in the industry—and they revolutionized how people pay for things. Online, on their devices, even at physical retail stores."

"What are they?"

"Well, I sold them," he said. "To Google. They did very little inside the app. They called them the best developed apps they'd ever bought." A hint of a smile wafted across Brian's face. "You know them as PayMe, PayHere, and PayWeb."

"You're kidding," Seren said. "Everyone uses PayMe. I bought a new pair of hiking boots with PayWeb this afternoon."

Brian nodded, because he knew exactly what she was saying. "I made over a billion dollars for each app," he said. "That's what Darren was saying I hadn't told you." He looked up, and he'd never seen Seren's eyes so wide.

"And now you work at Chestnut Ranch."

"Yes."

"You quit all that?"

"Yes," he said.

"Why?"

"Because of the ex-wife I told you about."

Seren's eyes got even wider. "Did she...? Was she...? What happened?"

Brian shook his head. "That's not really part of this story." He picked up his fork and scooped up another bite of pie. "My part—my secret—is that I'm really rich. I don't need to work at Chestnut Ranch for the money. In fact, Seth donates my paycheck to charity. I do it, because I love the slower pace of life. I love working with animals, and being outside, and not dealing with stress and meetings and other alphas who think they know more about my app than I do."

He put the pie in his mouth and looked at her, feeling very exposed. And he hadn't even told her about Cassie's cheating. He could save that for another night. He didn't need to reveal all of his secrets in one conversation.

"Your turn."

"Yours was a *good* secret," she said. "Mine's not."

"You said you'd tell me." Frustration began to rise within Brian. If she didn't tell him, then what? He'd ended things with her twice already, and he didn't think there'd be any coming back from a third time.

Not only that, but he didn't want to hang threats over her head every time she didn't tell him something. He knew how relationships worked, and bits and pieces of a person were revealed over time, as more trust was established.

"I didn't want to keep the relationship secret because of *you*," she said. "It has everything to do with *me*."

"Okay." It didn't feel like that to him, but Brian could deal with his self-consciousness at another time, by himself. "But it wasn't entirely because of Sorrell either."

"No." Seren shook her head. "Not entirely." She swept up another bit of whipped cream and licked it off her fork. Brian's hormones went into overdrive, and he commanded himself to calm down. They weren't anywhere near kissing status at the moment, facing off across a picnic table.

"I'm not good at this kind of stuff," she said again. "And I'm embarrassed of myself, that I'll mess it up. I mean, I've already messed up twice. So every time I see you, I think, 'what's he thinking? Is he thinking I'm so dumb because I don't know how to be a girlfriend?' You know?" She cocked her head, her eyes begging for him to understand.

"And then I mess up even more. I'm still not entirely convinced I am who you think I am, so I figured...I'll just see what happens. And you kept texting, and you kept calling, and you kept letting me dictate to you where you could park and where we could go. It was working for me, and I saw no reason to change it."

"Other than I wanted to change it," he said quietly.

"Yes. Other than that." She set her fork down, her eyes following it to the table. "I don't want to answer my sisters' questions. I don't want things to be complicated. I just want to keep living my normal life."

"And being with me complicates things." He wasn't asking, because he could hear what she was saying; he was merely rephrasing it.

"Yes. No." She looked up again. "No, of course not."

"But yes," he said. "Because now you have to answer questions. You have to wonder all the time what I see in you that you don't see in yourself. You have to think hard about something you haven't done very much and that you're worried about messing up."

She nodded. "It was easy to use Sorrell as a reason," she admitted. "And she *was* part of the reason."

Brian didn't know how to reassure Seren of his feelings. All he could do was say them and show them. She got to choose if she believed him or not. "Well, I can't help you with the sisters thing," he said. "I don't have any of those myself. But my brother did practically beat the information out of me that I was seeing you. Or rather, I told him about you after that first night at the homestead, and I asked him to help me get you back. Then you stopped by all by yourself." He gave her a smile she didn't look up to see.

"The only way you'll mess things up between us, Seren, is when you stop talking."

That got her to look up, a perfect brightness of hope in her eyes. "Really?"

"Really."

"Are you really a cowboy billionaire?"

"Yes," he said. "And you should also know that there are exactly two people who know that besides me and Tom."

"Who?"

"Well, three now. Darren, Seth, and you." He stared at her, hoping to drive home his point. "It's not something I want everyone to know."

"Why not?"

"I just don't," he said, sighing. "People...treat you different when they know you're rich."

"Do they?"

"If you don't, I'd be surprised."

"I won't," she said.

"I would hope not," Brian said. "Because I'm the same man I was when I got here this evening and you didn't know. The same man who parked down the lane and let you dictate where he could take you and pick you up. The money didn't change any of that."

She nodded and picked up her fork again. She took her first full bite of pie, and some of the tension surrounding them at the picnic table dissipated.

"I just have one more thing," Brian said, lifting his own fork.

Seren looked at him expectantly as she chewed her pie.

"If you're going to walk as fast as you did out here on our hike, I'm out." He grinned at her, waiting for her to hear the joke and laugh.

She finally did, and the sound was like a choir of angels singing to Brian's ears. He chuckled with her—until he heard the barking.

"That's Queen," he said, abandoning his pie and striding away from the picnic table. The dog barked and barked and barked, and it was not a pleasant sound. It was an aggressive, frightened sound, and Brian needed to find her quickly.

CHAPTER 12

S eren took off after Brian, her heart pounding in the back of her throat. "Queen?" she called, though Brian hadn't said the dog's name yet. It wasn't hard to find the German shepherd, because wow, Queen had a loud bark.

She trotted in a pacing stance, back and forth, back and forth at the far end of the garden, barking. Barking. Barking.

Seren turned toward Sarena and Darren as they came out of the house. Koda took off at a sprint toward the other dog, despite Darren's call to him. Everyone spilled out of the farmhouse now, all of them coming to the edge of the deck.

"What is it?" Stephen asked, and Seren looked past the backyard, past the garden and the chicken coops. She couldn't see anything.

Koda joined Queen, both of them having a contest on who could bark the loudest and the most.

Brian marched on, about halfway through the garden now. Sarena came down the steps. "Something's wrong."

Seren was inclined to agree. Two dogs losing their minds over nothing? She didn't think that would happen, especially for Queen, who'd always seemed so level-headed.

Darren followed Sarena, and so did Theo and Stephen, all of them with a similar gait as they strode out toward the dogs. Sorrell stayed on the deck, her hands running up and down her arms as if she were cold.

Seren climbed the steps to join her, because while she could do a few things around the ranch, she didn't know much. All at once, Brian stopped, pivoted, and came right back the way he'd been going.

"Bulls," he yelled, his voice carrying through the air, somehow above the barking of the dogs. Everyone else stopped walking out toward him too, and Sarena pointed to the right, where they could take a different way to get to a barn that housed ropes.

Brian went with them, never once checking to see where Seren was. Just before he disappeared behind the chicken coop, he looked her way and waved, and warmth gathered in her stomach and spread through her body.

"How many bulls do we have?" Sorrell asked, and Seren just looked at her.

It wasn't a funny question, but Seren laughed, because she needed to bleed the tension out of her body. "I have no idea," she said. "And you have no idea how happy it makes me that you don't know either."

Sorrell just looked at her with wide eyes, and Seren once again catalogued the differences between them. Sorrell worried *so much* about things, and Seren tended to laugh off her worries—especially if there was nothing she could do about them.

"They'll get them back in," Seren said, looking up again. Queen continued to pace, and as one enormous, black bull tried to step out from behind the stable, Seren suddenly knew why. "She's keeping them back there."

"She's cornered him," Sorrell said.

Koda manned Queen's right flank, flattening himself and barking, and Seren stepped to her left so she could see more clearly. "There's another one there," she said, pointing. "Koda's not letting him go anywhere."

"What's behind the stables?"

"Fences," Seren said. She knew that much, as she'd been out to the stables a couple of days ago to check on the gear she had to go horseback riding. She and Brian had never set a date to do it, and she didn't know if he'd have her over to Chestnut or if he'd want to come here. She figured she could at least be prepared, and she'd found the saddle she'd used in the past hanging on the wall, just waiting for her to return.

"The pasture," she added. "With some silos over on the left side there. They probably can't get through."

A horse's whinny filled the air, and the sound made Seren's blood chill. "Do you think they'll hurt the horses?"

"I hope not." Sorrell came to stand by Seren, and they both gazed out at the ranch. Through the shade, and with the summer shadows starting to cover everything, it really was made of gray and gold. Seren loved it, just as she'd loved growing up here.

She didn't have hayseed in her blood the way Sarena did,

but she loved the land where she'd been born and raised. A strong sense of Texas pride filled her, the same way it did every time she reached the summit of Enchantment Rock and looked out over the Texas Hill Country.

Calls from one person to the next reached her ears, and a moment later, Brian jogged out from between a couple of buildings and called Queen and Koda back. The dogs slinked to his side, giving the bulls about twenty more feet to venture out past the stables.

Seren saw movement on her left—Stephen was over there on horseback—and her right—Theo and Darren, also mounted with ropes coiled and ready in their hands.

She didn't see her sister—her pregnant sister—and she hoped Sarena was okay. "Bless her to be okay," she whispered.

"Amen," Sorrell added, and the two of them looked at each other. Understanding moved between them, and Sorrell put her arm around Seren's waist. "She's going to be okay."

"She's going to have to adjust what she does now that she's pregnant."

"You can be the one to tell her," Sorrell said.

"She doesn't hold back with me, you know."

"I know," Sorrell said. "That's why you should be the one to tell her."

"I'm sure Darren already has." Seren watched as nothing seemed to be happening. All the cowboys she could see were tensed, ready, and waiting. Even Brian.

"It's different coming from someone else," Sorrell said.

Before Seren could answer, a shriek ripped through the air, and a deafening crack followed. Both bulls came out from their hiding places, and Brian held out both hands to keep the dogs back.

Darren, Theo, and Stephen flew into action, throwing their ropes and catching their beasts. Sarena came running from behind the stable where the big, black bull had been, and her rope joined Stephen's around the animal's neck.

"Brian!" someone yelled, and he took a moment to turn toward the deck and command both dogs to go.

Queen listened to him immediately, lowering her tail as she ran toward Seren and Sorrell in a fast lope. Koda took another moment, then two. Theo yelled for Brian again, his footing slipping.

Sorrell gasped. Seren stuck her fingers in her mouth and whistled, which drew Koda's attention. "Come on!" she yelled, and the dog came toward her.

Brian turned and ran to the stable, dodging the bulls —literally dodging the black one as it lunged—and opening the doors. Ranch dogs rushed out of the opening, growling and barking as they started herding the bulls.

Sarena whistled at them, leading them like the pied piper toward the wider lane that would get the bulls back into their pen.

Watching dogs work was one of Seren's favorite activities, and she marveled at the ranch dogs, who only weighed thirty or forty pounds, as they wove in and around the bulls, snapping at them and keeping them moving where they needed to go.

Queen sat at her feet, her tongue hanging out of her

mouth, and Seren reached down to scratch her ears. "You're a smart one," she told the dog. "You thirsty?"

With the situation under control, she went inside and filled a big cooking bowl with water, bringing it out to the deck for Koda and Queen. They both drank noisily, which also made Seren happy.

"Where did you and Brian disappear to?"

Seren tensed with the question, but it was an easy one. "The picnic table." There, she'd confessed that she wasn't good enough to be with him, that she had no idea what she was doing as a girlfriend, and that she felt like an outsider all the time.

He hadn't laughed. He hadn't scolded her. He hadn't told her that her feelings were ridiculous.

"He's really nice," Sorrell said.

"He is," Seren agreed, because she knew her sister was talking about Brian.

"Really good-looking."

"Yes." Seren was fine agreeing with whatever Sorrell said. She could handle that. What she didn't want to talk about was how she felt. She didn't *know* how she felt.

"Do you get along with him?"

"Sometimes," Seren said, because it seemed like a lot of what had happened over the past couple of weeks wasn't exactly getting along. "When I'm not being stupid."

"You're not stupid," Sorrell said.

Seren just watched the ranch, waiting for everyone to come back. "I am when it comes to men," she finally said.

"You and me both."

She looked at Sorrell, who wore a look halfway between happy and sad. "He still hasn't asked?"

"I told you, I think I blew it with him."

"And I told you to go ask him." Seren didn't want to lecture Sorrell. "I took my own advice, by the way. That's why me and Brian got back together. I went to him."

"*Back* together?"

Seren nodded, because she'd have to come clean about last fall sooner or later. It might as well be sooner, then she wouldn't have to carry the guilt of telling half-truths to her sisters.

"When were—?"

"Can we at least wait until Sarena's with us?" Seren asked. "I don't want to have to explain everything twice."

Sorrell didn't say anything, and Seren had probably hurt her feelings. Exasperation slipped through her, because Seren's bluntness had hurt Sorrell plenty of times over the years. "Sorry, Sorrell," she murmured.

"It's fine," Sorrell said. "I wouldn't want to have to explain everything twice either."

"We'll help you with Theo," Seren said. "I know Sarena will. She used to talk to him all the time about you."

"I know," Sorrell said. "And I hated that, so I don't need your help."

Seren glanced at her sister, the power and bite in Sorrell's words quite uncharacteristic. "Okay," she said. "You can explain it all—once—when we're alone together, the three of us."

Sorrell nodded, took one last look at the ranch, and said, "I'm going to go clean up dinner."

Seren let her go, because Sorrell recovered by cleaning or cooking. She found her center again in the kitchen, and she liked to be alone while she did it. She looked at the dogs and said, "Come with me, guys."

They did what she said as if she were their master, and they followed her down the path to the picnic table where she and Brian had left their peach pie. She knew there was more inside, and Brian could have another whole piece. She didn't want hers, so she let the dogs eat the pie and lick the plates clean, enjoying how happy it made them.

With a new smile on her face, she said, "Let's go see if they're back yet." The dogs walked alongside her, clearly tired from their barking and holding back the bulls. Plus the peach pie binge.

They both took another drink of the water Seren had put on the porch for them, and she held open the back door so they could enter.

Everyone seemed to be talking at once, and Seren entered the farmhouse, the last to arrive. Her eyes sought out Brian, and he'd found her too. He rose from the table, which held a glass of water in front of him, and came toward her.

"Hey," she said. "You're okay."

"That was tense," he said, running his hands up her arms to her shoulders. His hands against her bare skin felt so good, and everything in Seren started tingling. "Good job getting Koda back." He smiled at her, held her gaze for a moment, and then dropped to a crouch in front of Queen.

"Aren't you the smartest dog ever?" He scrubbed her face and neck with his hands, and the dog clearly adored him. She hadn't stopped panting, and Seren wondered if German shepherds ever did. Brian praised her, and then moved on to Koda, whom Darren had already loved on.

Seren didn't know what happened next, but Sorrell had brought the pie to the table, as well as the coffee pot, and it seemed like everyone had gathered there again. Seren joined them, taking a chair beside Brian and waving off a piece of pie. Brian took one, and they talked.

Seren started to relax as she listened to their accounts of wrangling the bulls, and she was able to contribute a little bit too. The talk moved to the upcoming Chestnut Springs Fall Festival, and everyone started giving Sorrell suggestions for what she should enter for the baking competition.

After a while, Seren realized that she hadn't felt left out or alone once, and she smiled to herself. Maybe, with a little bit of effort, she didn't have to feel like an island or an outcast.

"Okay, time to wrap up this party," Sorrell said, standing. "Some of us have to go to work in the morning."

That caused an outcry from the cowboys, who definitely got up earlier than Sorrell did. Seren laughed with everyone, and she watched as Theo helped Sorrell while Stephen simply left the farmhouse. So Theo was definitely still interested in Sorrell; he just wasn't asking her to dinner anymore.

She wasn't sure how to say goodbye to Brian in a crowd, and she ended up slipping her hand in his and tugging him toward the front door.

"Brian," Darren said before they'd taken two steps. "Can

you come show me something on my laptop? It won't take but a few minutes."

"Sure." He looked at Seren and swept his lips across her cheek. "Call you later, okay?"

She froze with his physical touch. "Okay."

He went down the hall with Sarena and Darren, and Seren followed after them like a lost puppy. She paused halfway down the hall though, when she heard Sarena say to Darren, "Just don't wait up, that's all I'm saying."

"Sarena, you can't save everyone," Darren said. "And you need to rest after what happened tonight."

"Oh, I'm fine," Sarena said. "Now go on. I love you."

Seren walked forward then, making her footsteps obvious. Only Darren and Sarena loitered in the foyer, with the front door open. Darren left; Sarena lifted her hand and closed the door with a sigh.

When she turned back to Seren, she smiled. "All right," she said, coming toward her. She linked her arm through Seren's. "Time for some sister talk."

CHAPTER 13

S orrell Adams kept wiping the same spot of counter over and over, waiting for her sisters to say goodbye to their significant others. Whatever Sarena had said to Darren to get him to leave with Brian worked, because Seren and Sarena returned to the kitchen alone, arms linked together.

It took all of Sorrell's self-control not to glance at the back door, which Theo had walked through when he'd left a minute or two ago. He was always great to stay and help her clean up, and Seren wasn't so blind to relationships that she couldn't make herself scarce, giving Theo plenty of opportunity to ask Sorrell to dinner.

But he hadn't.

"All right," Sarena said. "My husband is concerned about this becoming an all-nighter, and I need to rest, and blah blah. So let's get talking." She rounded the couch and sat down, a sigh coming from her mouth. She wasn't showing at all yet, which Sorrell found surprising.

Her nerves reared up, but she left the washrag on the counter and joined her sisters in the living room. After perching on the coffee table in front of the couch and facing them, she took a deep breath.

"How are you feeling?" she asked Sarena, because she knew Seren wouldn't.

"Good," Sarena said, a falsely positive note in her voice. "I'm out of the first trimester, and I did have some morning sickness then."

"Are you really going to keep working the ranch?" Seren asked.

"Yes," Sarena said. "This is what I *do*, you guys." She frowned. "Darren asked the same thing."

"It wouldn't be the end of the world if you just...observed for a while," Sorrell said. She always worried about Sarena out on the ranch, sometimes reminding herself that her oldest sister hadn't gotten injured from ranch work. An ATV accident had been the cause of her lost foot, but ever since then, Sorrell had always taken an extra second in her nightly prayers to ask God to protect Sarena.

"I'm sure I will observe for a while," Sarena said. "How are we talking about me?" She shook her head and glared at Seren and then Sorrell, her expression softening. "Who wants to start?"

"Sorrell," Seren said quickly, and Sorrell's heart squeezed from front to back.

She swallowed. "All right," she said. "I don't need anyone

to take any action. I just want to state that up front." She looked back and forth between Seren and Sarena, who both looked at her like they didn't know what she was talking about.

They did, and everyone in the room knew it.

"I just want a little commiseration that Theo refuses to ask me out."

"Maybe you should ask him," Sarena said.

Sorrell's irritation spiked. "I said I didn't want any action."

"That's not action," Sarena argued. "It was a suggestion."

Sorrell sighed, beyond done with this day. She was grateful she got to sleep in her own bed, and that the farmhouse was nice and cool with the new air conditioner pumping along. But she didn't normally make three huge pizzas after work on a Thursday, and she had a big meeting in the morning. "Okay, I'm done."

"No, you can't be done," Seren said. "We're just starting."

"I'm done," Sorrell said, the tears starting to press against the backs of her eyes. "I don't want to talk about it anymore. I'll deal with Theo myself." She closed her mouth and looked at the others, practically daring them to say anything more about Theo Lange.

Sarena held her gaze for a moment, then turned to look at Seren. "You're up."

"What about me?" she asked. "What do you want to know? Lay it on me."

"I know you've been seeing him for longer than a week," Sarena said.

"Sort of," Seren said. "We...ahem, snuck around last fall."

"I knew it." Sarena looked absolutely gleeful, but Sorrell could feel Seren's discomfort. She managed to smile at her younger sister, mostly to keep her talking.

"It was fun," Seren said. "I liked him, but I was...worried about a lot of things." She cleared her throat. "The pact I'd made with Sorrell, for one. And a few more issues I'm still dealing with."

"Pact with Sorrell?" Sarena swiveled her head between the two of them.

"Not tonight," Sorrell said. "Keep going, Seren. What are you still dealing with?"

"My own insecurities," she said, keeping her eyes on her hands in her lap. "He kissed me a couple of weeks ago, I guess, and he didn't laugh. So that helped a little bit."

"He kissed you already?" Sarena's eyes grew wide, and Sorrell wanted to reach out and slap her knee. Couldn't she see Seren just needed to talk?

"He wanted to last fall, but I was afraid," Seren whispered. "And then he texted at your vow renewal, and we met up that afternoon. *I* actually kissed him then. It was...amazing." She flicked her eyes up, but she didn't settle her gaze on anything.

Sorrell exchanged a glance with Sarena, wishing she were half so bold as their youngest sister. She couldn't even imagine sneaking off to meet Theo, and the initiating a kiss...? She would never do it.

She reached out and touched her knee. Seren finally raised her eyes to Sorrell's, and the moment turned pure. "It was amazing?"

"So amazing," Seren said. "I like him a lot. I think he likes me. He keeps saying he does. I don't get it, though. I don't get how I could be so bad with men in the past, or how Pierce could literally laugh at me when he kissed me, and Brian... doesn't." She looked from Sarena to Sorrell, who wanted to wrap her in a hug and tell her Pierce was a tool and Brian a gentleman. A real cowboy, who loved the land and loved horses, and just wanted a good woman at his side.

Seren was that good woman, even if she didn't know it.

"You've got nothing to worry about," Sarena said kindly. "Of course he likes you. I've always wondered why you didn't have a thousand men knocking on the door. You're smart, and skinny, and tall. You have great skin, and beautiful hair, and you don't shy away from anything." She tossed a glance at Sorrell, a clear indication she wanted her to jump in.

"I scare men," Seren said. "I'm too blunt, and I don't have, I don't know, the right kind of feelings."

"What does that mean?" Sorrell asked.

"It means you cry over stuff, Sorrell. Which is fine. You cry over stuff people are supposed to cry over. I don't. I don't know how to tell a man how I'm feeling, because I just compartmentalize it all away." She shook her head. "This part doesn't matter. I'm not worried about this part yet."

"What are you worried about?" Sarena said.

"That I'll mess it all up," she said. "I don't know how to be a girlfriend. I've literally never done it before." She went back to picking her nails and staring at her hands. "Like tonight, I didn't know how to introduce him. I didn't know what to say. So I said nothing, and it's awkward, and he ends up fending for himself, basically. Because I'm clueless." Her misery poured off of her in waves, and Sorrell's mouth turned down.

"You'll figure it out," Sarena said. "I didn't know how to be a fake wife, and I figured that out."

A beat of silence filled the house, and then Seren scoffed. Then she laughed, and Sorrell let herself giggle too.

"Yeah, and now you're a real wife," Sorrell said.

"Right, exactly," Sarena said. "So just keep being his girl-friend, and you'll figure it out, and then you'll be really good at it."

"You think so?" Seren asked.

"Yes," Sorrell and Sarena said together. They exchanged a glance while Seren wasn't watching, and much more was said.

"Okay," Seren said. "I'll do my best."

"That's all anyone can ask," Sarena said.

Both Sorrell and Seren looked at her, and she asked, "What?"

"You sounded like Dad just then," Seren said.

Sorrell started to nod, because what Sarena had just said had come out of their father's mouth plenty of times over the years. "You really did." Her chest squeezed, and those tears came, and Sorrell knew she was the most emotional sister. Sometimes the others treated her like a delicate flower, one made of glass that could break at any time.

How she wished she could be strong and intimidating like Seren. Or capable and confident like Sarena. But she was just mousy Sorrell, who wore pantsuits to the community center, attended meetings, made no difference in the world, and came home at the end of the day only to have to do it all again the next morning.

"I miss him," she said, thinking of their father.

Seren reached out and squeezed her hand. "So do I."

Sarena took Seren's hand in one of hers, and Sorrell's in the other. "As do I."

"We should do something next month," Sorrell suggested. "Even just take flowers out to his and Mama's graves. Fifteen minutes in the evening, after work." She searched her sister's faces, hoping to find acceptance there.

Thankfully, she did, and they both nodded.

That decided, Sorrell got up. "Okay, I have a meeting in the morning. I love you guys." She waited for them to stand, and she hugged them both before grabbing her phone off the kitchen counter and retreating to her room.

Seren would walk Sarena down the lane to the second farmhouse now on the property, and they'd talk a little more. Hopefully, Sarena would remind Seren that she shouldn't give up on Brian just because it was hard or outside her comfort zone. Seren had a tendency to do that—just like Sorrell had a tendency to sit back and let life happen to her.

"No more," she muttered as she perched on the edge of her bed and swiped on her phone. She wasn't quite brave enough to call Theo, but she was a darn good texter.

Before she lost her brief window of determination and confidence, she tapped out a message, read over it, and sent it.

Now she just had to wait and see what Theo said back.

CHAPTER 14

Theo Lange finished his pullups and wiped his forehead. He really needed to get a treadmill, because it was too hot to run outside in the summer, even if he got up at four a.m. He had to do something to drive Sorrell Adams from his mind every morning and night, or he'd go mad.

Most days, he felt like his brain was already addled. "Because you can't stay away from her."

He knew his muttered words to himself were true, and he sat down at the computer in his living room, shaking the mouse to get it going. He'd been looking at the job boards for other ranches, because he needed a change of pace. He'd enjoyed being here at Fox Hollow, but Sarena expected a lot of him and Stephen, and Theo had been willing to give it.

Now...now he felt like he needed something else in his life. He didn't need a job at all, and he figured he might as well love the one he had. The truth was, Theo didn't love being at Fox Hollow the way he once had.

While his heart rate settled after his sit-ups, push-ups, and pullups, he typed in the search terms he'd put in a dozen times before and waited for the website to generate the results.

Rootbeer—that one had been up for six months. Theo wasn't interested in being the only hired help, because that sounded like a situation he was already in. Small family operation, without much to offer a career cowboy. They'd do better just to find a young man in town who needed a few extra bucks and didn't mind working fourteen hours a day.

Theo minded, especially now that he'd turned forty. He didn't mind getting up early, but he wanted to be off early too. There were big ranches around that had a dozen or more cowboys to work the eighteen-hour days in shifts.

"The Singer Ranch," he read aloud, his pulse picking up again. This was a new listing, and someone would have to be completely outside the cowboy culture in Texas to not know about the Singers.

He clicked on the listing, seeing that it had been made only seven hours earlier. He hurried to apply, because The Singer Ranch was exactly what he'd been looking for as he'd logged onto this job board for the past several months.

That done, he leaned back in his chair and exhaled. "If possible, Lord," he whispered. "I'd like to get a position with the Singers."

They'd pay better than Fox Hollow, and he wouldn't have to work as much. Both of those were positives, but Theo knew the real issue was seeing Sorrell every blasted day. Even when he went out of his way *not* to see her, he still did. She texted or he had to run into the house real quick—and the evidence of Sorrell was everywhere there.

She'd made it clear that he had no shot with her, and he was tired of feeling like a foolish sap, hanging on to the beautiful woman. If she didn't want him, Theo needed to try to find someone who did.

He clicked back on the screen, navigating to his online investment accounts. He checked these every night too, and sometimes every morning. He'd learned the habit from his biological father, whom he'd only known for thirteen months before the man had passed away. Harvey checked his money multiple times during the day, and it had taken Theo some time before he'd realized he didn't need to be as obsessed as Harvey.

He had no full siblings, and sometimes Theo felt completely alone in the world. When he checked his money, though, he could feel Harvey's presence right there over his shoulder, looking at the numbers and whispering advice.

He'd inherited a lot of money from his father, and he'd applied the investment advice the old man had given him before he'd died. Theo had taken his three hundred million, and over the course of a decade had increased it four-fold.

He could still remember the day the accounts had ticked from eight figures to nine, and he'd sworn he could hear his father saying, *You're a billionaire now, boy. Don't ever go back.*

And Theo had been determined to do exactly that. Never go back below nine figures in his bank account.

Tonight, he still had that many, and in fact, several of his stocks had gone up in value. He scrawled the numbers in his notebook next to his mousepad, flipping a few pages to see what the historic highs and lows were for the stocks he owned.

He contemplated selling every single day, but tonight, he made the decision to hold onto everything he had for another day. One of his investments, one of the largest airlines in the world, was reaching its historic high, and last time they'd done that, they'd reorganized the board, split their stocks, and their market shares had gone down by a third.

He'd put his ear to the Internet over the weekend and see if he could find anyone talking about Continental. Then he'd know if he should sell while they were this high or if he should hold.

Satisfied he could go to bed now, he powered down his computer and picked up his phone. A glance at it showed someone had texted. Probably Sarena. She'd either thanked him again for helping with the bulls or she'd given him a special assignment for tomorrow.

His first inclination was to ignore it until morning, because he just wasn't in the mood to think about work. He glanced at the dark computer screen, wishing he'd hear from the Singers by morning.

In the end, he wasn't the type of man to ignore his boss, and Sarena would like a confirmation before she went to bed. Theo swiped open his phone and tapped on his texts. He just had the one, and it wasn't from Sarena.

"Sorrell," he said, reading quickly.

Hey, Theo, I was just wondering—have I ruined everything between us?

His heart flipped over, now in the wrong position in his chest. Confusion immediately followed, and his thumbs flew over the screen, tapping out a message almost without instruction from his brain.

I don't know what you mean. Why would you have ruined everything between us?

He'd left the homestead less than an hour ago—what had changed? When he'd left her in the kitchen, she'd grinned at him and thanked him for helping with the dishes, same as always. On nights like tonight, where they'd spent a lot of time together, and things were easy and good between them, Theo thought about asking her to dinner. Again.

After her last rejection, which had come on her blasted birthday, while he held roses in his hands, he'd promised himself he wouldn't. He'd asked her out more times than he could count, and she'd turned him down every single time. Every single one. He wasn't going to do it again. He had one shred of pride left, and it was the only thing getting him through each day.

Oh, good, Sorrell said. *I'm glad. Night, Theo.*

He looked up, more confused than ever. When he felt like this, he always did the same thing—he called his mother. She lived on the Carolina coast, so it was getting late there, and he quickly got the line ringing between them.

"Theo, dear," she said by way of hello.

Just the sound of her voice ironed some things flat in Theo's soul. "Hey, Ma."

"What time is it there? Why aren't you in bed?"

"I got a strange text from Sorrell." His mother knew all about Sorrell, as Theo had told her everything over the years.

"What did she say?"

Theo read the text to her, as well as his response, and Sorrell's. "So what is she talking about?"

"Theo, dear, this woman wants you to ask her out."

"No," Theo said, shaking his head. "You're wrong about that, Ma. I did, remember? A bunch of times."

"When was the last time?"

"Oh, shoot, I don't know." He exhaled, trying to go back in time. "Months now."

"You don't think something has changed for her in those months?"

"No," Theo said. "I don't." Sorrell hadn't been acting any different around him in that time. She hadn't said anything different. She'd done absolutely nothing different that would lead him to believe she'd say yes if he asked her to dinner one more time.

"I think she's probably asking if she's ruined things between you by saying no."

"Well, maybe she has." He thought of The Singer Ranch, but he didn't want to tell his mother about it until he knew if he had a new position or not.

"That's why she was asking," his mom said. "And you told her no, things were fine. So my guess is she's glad, because she's expecting you to ask her out again—and Theo, this time she's going to say yes."

"You really think so?"

"Maybe she's ready to say yes."

Theo had no response, because he could not imagine what Sorrell saying yes would sound like. She'd literally never told him yes when he'd asked her out. She said yes to other things, so she knew and could say the word.

He just didn't think she'd say it to the one question he wanted her to.

"Okay," he said, his voice full of doubt. "Thanks, Ma. I have to get to bed."

"I'll say," his mother said. "You're never up this late."

"Love you," Theo said, and his mother repeated the words back to him. He checked his phone just to make sure Sorrell hadn't added anything to the conversation while he'd been on the phone with his mother. She hadn't, and Theo went down the hall to the only bathroom in the tiny cowboy cabin.

He brushed his teeth, changed into pajamas, and knelt to say his prayers. Once he was in bed, the covers bunched up down by his feet because it was too hot to sleep with them over him, he thought of Sorrell.

Maybe she was ready to say yes, but was he ready for her to say yes?

He'd just decided to move on and find a new job at a new ranch. "You should leave it alone," he said to himself in the darkness. It was with that thought in his head that he finally fell asleep, his personal vow not to ask Sorrell out again renewed.

CHAPTER 15

Brian stepped out of the brutal heat and into the homestead at Chestnut Ranch. Not only did the air conditioning work, but the scent of chocolate and peppermint hung in the air, even back here in the mudroom. "Hello?" he called, because Janelle had been working from home some days this summer, and he'd run into her and the girls during his checks on the progress of the remodel.

No one answered him today, though. He walked into the kitchen and found a plate of fudgy cookies with white morsels in them. *Peppermint chocolate cookies*, the sign read, in Kelly's handwriting.

Without hesitation, Brian unwrapped the plate and picked up a cookie, taking a bite as he started looking around. The new windows seemed to let in even more light, because they were so darn clean. Brian liked the new design for opening, and he went over and opened the window without a hitch. He quickly closed it, because it was far too hot to leave a window open.

The hardware would go in after the painting, and that was starting tonight. He thought of Seren, and the gallons of paint they'd picked up the previous night. She'd needed his truck, and he'd been more than happy to escort her to town to get the paint. Russ and Janelle had gone with her suggestion of Chantilly Lace for the color, and he'd never seen anyone so excited about paint in his life.

He smiled, because the last month with Seren had been amazing. One of the best of his life, at least since the last time they'd been seeing each other, and before that, he had to go all the way back to the sale of his apps to find the kind of happiness he currently had in his life.

Queen whined, and Brian turned back to her, remembering he'd promised her a drink in the homestead. He opened cupboards until he found a big bowl, which he filled with filtered water from the sink. She lapped at it enthusiastically while Brian went into the living room to see how the remodel was going there.

This room was ready for painting, as was the dining room and kitchen. The floor just needed to be finished in the living room, and he'd been promised it would be done that afternoon. Upstairs, a couple of the rooms had been emptied, and these were ready for painting too.

Seren had estimated two weeks of painting in the evenings, and he'd asked her if there was any way to take time off from her day job and focus on the homestead during the day. That way, Russ and Janelle wouldn't be home, and she'd have way more time.

She'd asked her boss, and she'd only gotten one week.

He'd talked to Seth, and he'd given him permission to work on the homestead around his normal chores. Together, he and Seren were planning to get the work done in seven days. He was tired thinking about that, but also excited. More time with Seren was always good in his book.

He started down the steps, hearing the front door open and people come inside. They talked to each other, and he slowed as they moved in front of him. "Oh, hey, Brian," Evan said as he passed. "We'll be done in probably two or three hours."

"Perfect," Brian said, smiling at the man and the two that followed him. "I was just checking on things for paint. She's coming tonight."

"Should be ready for her," Evan said.

"Who is it?" one of the other guys, Tony, asked. "We've got another project whose painter has ghosted them, and everyone is so busy right now."

"Yeah, summer seems to be the time to get work done on your house," Evan said.

"It's because summer is the best time to sell," Tony said. "That's what's happening here. She wants her house painted before she lists it."

"It's Serendipity Adams," Brian said. "But I don't think she'd take on another project. She only does painting on the side, and she had to take work off to do this."

"Can't hurt to ask her," Tony said. "I know the Adams."

Everyone did, it seemed. They had lived in the Chestnut Springs area for a long, long time. Brian just nodded, and he faced the big windows at the back of the house. "All right, well, I have to get back to the ranch." He didn't want to go very badly, but he snagged another cookie and headed out the back door, leaving Evan and his crew to finish the flooring.

Hours later, he'd showered, oiled his beard, and eaten dinner before telling Queen, "All right, girl. Let's go see what Seren needs help with."

Normally, he'd walk down the road, enjoying the evening air and the golden hue of the sky. But he told himself he could do both of those things from behind the wheel of his truck, with the air conditioning blowing, and Queen loaded up in the back for the quick drive.

Russ's truck wasn't in the driveway, and Brian wondered which brother they'd gone to stay with for the week. Probably Seth, as he had the most room and lived so very close to the ranch that Russ ran.

Before he even got to the front door, he could hear the music pounding inside. He smiled to himself, because this eighties rock was so Seren. He opened the front door and nearly got blasted with an electric guitar riff.

"Seren," he called, but he didn't have to go far to find her. She came through the arched doorway as he closed the front door behind him, a rag and a paintbrush in her hand.

"Oh, hey," she said, and Brian drank her in. Every time he saw her, she was like a tall glass of cold water to his parched throat. Tonight, she wore a pair of shorts the color of denim but they weren't denim and a gray T-shirt with old paint splattered on it.

She was stunning.

"Hey." He grinned at her. "Just me and you tonight."

She smiled back and extended the paintbrush toward him. "Let me turn down the music." She returned to the kitchen with the brush still in her hand, and Brian followed her. She adjusted the volume on her speaker, and when she turned, Brian was right there in front of her.

He hadn't kissed her in a long time, and he wondered if tonight would be the night. It was almost like they'd started over when they'd gone for pizza in town. The kiss from the stargazing night had been in the back of his mind, teasing him, but he hadn't made another move since then.

"We'll start in the front room," she said. "It should go fast. Then move in here. Get the basement done as quickly as we can." She pressed the paintbrush to his chest, and Brian covered her hand with his.

"Sounds good." he stepped out of the way and let her lead him back into the front room.

"We need to tape it all," she said. "The ceiling color isn't changing."

"Lucky for us," he said. "Hey, did Tony call you today?"

"He left a message," Seren said. "I was on the way down the rock with a group." She climbed up on a ladder and started taping the ceiling. "You can start with that other roll."

Brian did, hoping he was doing a good enough job. He didn't paint very often, but Seren looked at his green lines and nodded. "All right." She turned to the industrial-sized bucket. "Now we paint."

She opened it and stood back. "I need your muscles to pour that, cowboy." She grinned at him, and Brian chuckled as he lifted the big bucket and poured the paint into two trays. It was glorious and beautiful as it flowed into the tray, the sharp scent of it actually comforting to Brian.

"I love paint," Seren said, and he looked at her to find her admiring the trays too. "Do you want high or low?"

"Definitely high," he said.

She handed him the roller with an extendable handle and picked up a regular one. "Let's do this." She loaded her roller while he did the same, and they began to roll the new color over the old. Since it was also white, they didn't need to prime, and the new paint slicked on easily.

Seren sang along with the music, and Brian simply enjoyed listening to her voice as she tripped over some words but nailed others.

She was much faster than him, but he worked steadily to catch up to her. "How are things at the park?" He glanced at her to judge her reaction, because sometimes Seren didn't like talking about her job.

"It's busy," she said. "I feel bad taking time off." She smiled though. "But it will be nice to have some time off, and its air conditioned here."

"That is nice," he said.

"Mm." She stood back. "You're kind of slow, Mister Gray."

"Oh-ho," he said. "I'm making sure I do it right."

"Yeah, okay." She giggled and crowded into his space to work on the section of wall he stood in front of.

"This roller is harder to use," he said. "I have to stand way back here."

"We can switch." She came toward him, her dark chocolate eyes glinting with a grin. She held out the roller, sliding it right down his chest. "Oops."

Brian sucked in a breath and looked down at the bumpy path of white paint on his blue shirt. "Oops? You did that on purpose."

She laughed, tipping her head back, and Brian grabbed onto the roller. She squealed and tried not to give it to him. He managed to get it from her, and he ran it right down her bare arm.

"Hey," she said, surprise in those pretty eyes. "I didn't get it on your skin."

"Yeah, you ruined my shirt. That'll at least wash off." He liked whatever game this was, and before he knew it, she'd swiped her fingers through the wet paint on her arm and wiped it down his cheek.

"Oh, you're dead," he said, turning to the tray. He had no idea what he was going to do, but he abandoned the roller and moved his fingers through the pool of paint.

"Brian," she said, half laughing while she stared at his fingers. "Don't."

He advanced toward her, and she kept backing up until her back met the front door. "Don't," she said again, her voice turning a bit hard.

Brian's fingers dripped with paint, and he took another step toward her. "You started it."

"And you can be the bigger person and end it," she said.

"Mm hm." He reached out and grabbed the hem of her shirt. She yelped as he knotted his fingers in the fabric, using it to wipe them fairly clean. He put his other hand on her waist and when she looked up at him, he lowered his head and kissed her.

It had been far too long since he'd done this, and he noticed as she melted into him, her hands coming up and threading through his hair, sliding down his face, and finally settling on his shoulders.

He pulled away, his breathing quicker now. "How's that for an ending?"

"Good," she whispered, stretching up to kiss him again.

CHAPTER 16

Seren had forgotten how wonderful it was to kiss Brian, and he'd pulled away far too soon. She didn't care if they got a bit behind schedule. Kissing him was worth it. She gripped his collar and kept him right where she wanted him, and when she was finally satisfied, she leaned back into the door, severing their connection.

She breathed in deep through her nose, getting the scent of paint, Brian's skin, and his cologne. He smelled like musk and male, and Seren sure did like it.

"Seren?"

"Yeah?" She opened her eyes to find Brian hadn't backed up at all, not even an inch. "Do you want children?"

Surprise flowed through her. "Um, I don't know."

"I think you do." He ducked his head and curled a lock of her hair around one of his fingers. "I figure maybe it's time we started talking about some serious things."

Seren thought they'd talked about several serious things

already. Mostly her issues, though he still hadn't mentioned why he'd sold his apps and given up his life in Seattle. She hadn't given a ton of thought to his financial situation, and their relationship the past month or so had been the easiest it had ever been.

"I've never thought of myself as a mother," Seren said. "I'm not very nurturing."

"I think that might be one of those self-perceptions that's just not true."

"I want to be honest," she said, pulling in a breath as his lips landed on her neck. "And that's how I've always felt. I think I'd say I wanted kids, simply because women are supposed to want kids, right?"

"It's okay if you don't," he said, pulling back.

Her skin felt chilled and heated at the same time. She looked into his eyes and asked, "Do you want children?"

"I wouldn't mind them," he said. "Especially if they can cook like Kelly." He smiled, and it was so genuine and soft, Seren fell a little bit more in love with him.

"I wouldn't count on that," she said. "Remember I said Sorrell's the one with all the cooking genes?"

"I can cook decently enough," he said.

"You can?" She raised her eyebrows and studied his face.

"Want to come to dinner at my cabin this week? We can work here during the day, and I'll cook for you."

"Sure," she said.

"Great." He backed up, removing his touch from her body. She hadn't realized her shirt had ridden up on her waist until his warm skin wasn't against hers. "Let's finish this and then see what Kelly left us for a treat."

"It looked like apple pie," Seren said. "And she said there was cinnamon whipped cream in the fridge."

"Sounds amazing."

"I think I know the way to your heart," she said with a laugh. "Through your stomach."

He chuckled with her, but he didn't deny it. They finished the room, and Seren was glad the conversation had gotten started, even if it was with a harder topic. She hadn't minded just listening to the music while they worked either, and she realized how comfortable she was with Brian.

She wasn't constantly worried she wasn't good enough for him, or what she should say to him. A new sense of warmth moved through her, because this was further than she'd ever gotten in a relationship before—and further in her own self-love.

"Apple pie," Brian said later, during their break. "You were right." He got out the whipped cream and added, "What's your favorite dessert?"

"My mother used to make this chocolate pie," Seren said. "Sorrell has the recipe and we have it for Thanksgiving every year. And on my mother's birthday."

He nodded and cut her a sliver of pie. He nudged the whipped cream closer to her, and she put a little dollop on her treat. "We're doing a ceremony for my father next week," she said. "Would you like to come?"

He looked up, surprise in his eyes. "When?"

"Wednesday," she said. "The date of his death." Sudden

sadness moved through Seren, and she tried to smile. It shook on her face, and Brian gathered her into his arms.

"Hey, it's okay," he whispered, his body so stable. His arms were so strong around her. She leaned on him, disliking this feeling of weakness but enjoying that he was with her to support her through it. "I'll come."

"Thanks," she said. "Darren will be there, and I think Sorrell invited Stephen and Theo."

Brian nodded, stroking her hair in a tender, loving way. The moment between them felt real and powerful, and Seren wanted to hold onto the memory of it for a long time.

She eventually stepped back and opened a drawer to find a fork. Brian said nothing else, and they ate their pie with the radio playing background music.

"Let's see what else we can do tonight," he said once they'd finished.

"I bet we can do the little hallway into here," she said. "And maybe up the stairs." She followed him into the front room to get back to work, feeling more loved and accepted than she ever had before.

* * *

The following week, Seren stopped at the florist to pick up the bouquets she'd ordered for the small graveside service she and her sisters had put together for their father. Sorrell had texted to say she could get them, as she'd been too upset to go to work.

Seren had ordered them, and they wouldn't be ready until

four o'clock. By then, she was on her way home from work, so there was no reason for Sorrell to drive into town. She'd ordered three bouquets, one for each sister, and another small bouquet of roses so the cowboys that were coming with them could have something to lay on the ground too.

She managed to smile and thank the woman, pay for the flowers, and get them all out to her car. Her chest hitched as something pulled tight through it, and she wept quietly on the way back to the farmhouse. She cried so rarely that when she did, it was something serious—or she was so stressed out that she couldn't handle one more thing.

She supposed mourning the passing of her father was something serious, but she still wiped her eyes and gave herself a few minutes before going inside so her tears wouldn't be so obvious.

"She's here," Sorrell said once Seren had closed the front door. Her sister met her in the hallway, and it was clear she'd been crying. She probably had been all day. Sorrell swept her into a hug as if Seren were several hours late and Sorrell was relieved to find her alive.

"What's wrong?" she asked, because this didn't feel like a regular hug.

"Uncle Dale had to go to the hospital today." Sorrell stepped back and wiped her eyes.

"Oh, no. Why?" Though the girls didn't get along particularly well with their uncle, that bridge had started to mend last fall, when Sarena had learned why Uncle Dale and their father hadn't gotten along. They'd both been married to the girls' mother, and there was a lot of history between the brothers.

"They think he has the flu."

"In July?"

"And he's older, and he's got a compromised respiratory system." She turned and led the way back into the house. "We're going to go visit him after our service."

Seren juggled the flowers as she followed her sister. In the living room, she found her aunt and cousins, and she was glad she'd gotten the extra bouquet. She put all the floral stuff on the counter and turned to say hello.

"Hi, Aunt Scottie." She embraced her aunt, who hugged her tight. "Regina. RonniJean." She hugged them both as well. "Thanks for coming."

"We came to tell you about Uncle Dale," Aunt Scottie said. "But Sarena said we could come to the little service y'all planned."

"Of course," Seren said. She was proud of herself for how diplomatic she was being. The doorbell rang, and she glanced at the clock.

"That'll probably be Brian. Excuse me."

"Who's Brian?" Aunt Scottie asked as Seren walked away. "He got invited when we didn't?"

"He's my boyfriend," Seren said over her shoulder, ignoring the gasps from her cousins. Regina and RonniJean had never hurt for dates to the prom, that was for sure.

Seren opened the front door to find Brian there, and she stepped right into his arms, needing his strength and support. "Hey." He held her right against his chest, and Seren liked being there.

"My aunt and cousins are here," she said, stepping back. "Sorry."

He smiled. "I can handle an aunt."

"We'll see," she said, taking his hand and leading him back into the living room. "Aunt Scottie, Regina, and RonniJean, this is Brian Gray." She beamed up at him. "My boyfriend. Brian, my aunt Scottie, and her daughters Regina and RonniJean."

"So nice to meet you," Brian said, reaching up and taking off his cowboy hat.

"And you," Aunt Scottie said, her chin lifting slightly.

"Let's eat," Sorrell said. "Now that everyone's here. Then we can go out to the grave, and then the hospital."

"Hospital?" Brian asked, squeezing Seren's hand.

"My uncle had to go to the hospital, I guess," she said. "He has the flu and had trouble breathing."

"Oh, that's too bad."

Seren faced Sorrell, who had put a bunch of their freezer food in the oven. "French fries," she said. "Baked chicken. Come eat."

Even freezer food was better when Sorrell made it, because she put some magical spice on the French fries, and she'd mixed together barbecue sauce and mayo for a dipping sauce. It felt odd to be socializing and eating like normal on this day.

Once they were all seated at the table, Seren said, "Let's say something about Dad." She looked at Sorrell and Sarena. "If you knew him. I mean, I know Brian didn't know him."

"Neither did I," Darren said.

"The rest of us can say something," Aunt Scottie said.

"What a great idea, Serendipity." She started, going on and on about her brother and how great he was with horses. She sniffled and wiped her eyes, and Seren once again felt everything inside her crumbling.

She embraced the emotions, because they made her feel human. She didn't have to compartmentalize this pain to deal with later, behind a closed door, by herself. She could let it out and not have to worry.

So she did.

* * *

"I love you, Daddy," she said later, after dinner and after the somber walk out to the family graveyard. Her mother was there too, right at his side. Seren bent down and placed her flowers on the ground in front of the headstone.

Everyone said something and put down a flower, and then Brian said, "Would you like someone to say a prayer?"

"Yes," Sarena said, retreating to Darren's side and linking her arm through his. "That's a nice idea, Brian. Would you?"

He took his cowboy hat off and held it against his chest, and Seren wished she had a camera so she could take a picture of this single moment in time. She couldn't close her eyes though everyone else did.

"Dear Lord," Brian said, his voice deep and filled with power and grace. "We thank Thee for this opportunity to gather as friends and family to remember a man that was clearly loved. Bless this ground where he sleeps and bless those that live and work at this ranch with comfort and a measure of Thy peace."

He opened his eyes and met Seren's. "Amen," he said.

"Amen," everyone else chorused, but Seren couldn't get her voice to work. Sorrell cried and turned away, heading back to the farmhouse with Stephen and Aunt Scottie. Seren should've been surprised Theo wasn't right at her sister's side, but she was still sorting through her own emotions when it came to Brian.

He enveloped her in a hug, and he kept his arm around her as he turned her and they started back to the farmhouse too. "Thanks for inviting me to this. It was really nice."

"Thanks for coming," she said, her voice a little rusty. "That was a really nice prayer."

He nodded, and Seren wondered what being in love felt like. Was it warm and comfortable? Was it this feeling coursing through her veins and making her heart beat in a way it never had before? Was it watching a man pray for her and feeling like she didn't want to be anywhere else?

She didn't know, and that confused her. She also worried that she was the only one feeling these things, so she kept them all bottled tight, determined not to let them out until she was alone and could deal with her feelings and questions in private.

CHAPTER 17

Brian finished tying the big, red bow on the front door of the homestead as Russ's truck eased into the driveway. He'd just spent an hour inside, making sure every pillow sat in exactly the right spot, and ensuring there wasn't any leftover sawdust or painter's tape in the house.

The remodel was done, and Brian was relieved. He'd thought he'd enjoy a break from the ranch work, but managing contractors, installations, and the budget wasn't something he wanted to do again.

"Hey," Russ called as he got out of the truck. "You ready for us?"

"Yes," Brian called back. "Come on up."

The girls came up the steps first, but Brian wouldn't let them inside until Russ and Janelle arrived. "I think you're going to love it," he said.

"Anything is going to be better than what it was," Janelle said. But she was clearly nervous—and opinionated.

Brian reminded himself that he hadn't designed what had been done inside the house. He'd simply executed her vision for the homestead. "Without making you wait any longer," he said. "Who wants to pull the bow and go in first?"

"I do!" Kadence said, raising her hand and bouncing on the balls of her feet.

"All right," he said, beaming at her. "Go for it."

Kadence stepped forward and pulled on the end of the bow to release it. She opened the door and stepped inside, saying, "Wow," in an awed voice. Brian hoped they'd all have a child-like reaction to the homestead, and he stayed out of the way as they all went inside.

He took a deep breath and followed them, so he could explain anything they had questions about.

"This paint color is perfect," Janelle said. "I had my doubts, but I can admit I was wrong."

Russ grinned as he looked around the front room. "It's great."

"These are those expensive curtains," Brian said. "Not exactly the same fabrics as what you'll see in the living room, but the same colors."

"The floors are amazing," Russ said, toeing the ground.

"So I was right about that." Janelle shot him a smile, and Russ returned it. They went into the kitchen, and Janelle shrieked. It sounded happy to Brian, and he smiled as he followed them.

Janelle touched everything from the cupboards to the new appliances to the curtains in the living room. "Look at this couch."

It was huge—absolutely huge—and had been custom-built into a sectional that could seat twelve adults. Since Russ and Janelle hosted so many family events at the homestead, they'd wanted a lot of seating. They'd gotten it.

"I love this," Janelle said.

"New paint everywhere," Brian said. "Upstairs and in the mudroom."

"In my room?" Kadence asked, already heading for the stairs.

"All rooms," Brian said.

"This is really amazing," Russ said. "Thank you for managing all of this, Brian."

"My pleasure," he said. "You guys did all the hard work of choosing everything."

"Ooh, look at the rug," Janelle said, still inspecting every element. She glanced up, loads of happiness in her face. "And yes, thank you, Brian."

"Mom?" Kelly asked. "Can I make peanut butter cookies in the new oven?"

"Of course," Janelle said.

As much as Brian wanted a plate of cookies, he also wanted to go home. "Are we good here?"

"Yes," Russ said, stepping over to shake Brian's hand. "Thank you again."

"Anytime." Brian smiled and headed out, ready for dinner and an hour of dog training. Then maybe he'd put something on TV and fall asleep on the couch.

July had gone, and August had arrived, but the heat seemed perpetual. It just went on and on, and it was these endless summer days that made Brian consider moving back to Seattle. At least then he'd get to experience a cold rain instead of the constant warmth, even when it rained.

The ceremony at the graveyard at Fox Hollow Ranch had been really nice, and Brian had thought he and Seren had been getting along really well.

But their relationship had slowed to a crawl over the past couple of weeks. He'd only seen her a couple of times since then, and even their texted conversations had slowed down. Brian could feel her putting distance between them, but he was too tired to confront her on it.

Maybe now that the remodel was finished. "Or maybe not," he mumbled to himself as he pulled in front of his house. Queen lay on the porch, right where he'd left her an hour ago.

He didn't want to constantly pursue Seren, because he was starting to think he liked her more than she liked him. He didn't want to feel like he was forcing her into a relationship she didn't want.

He didn't text her when he went inside the cabin. He left his phone in his pocket and picked up the bag of dog treats. "Come on, Queen," he said, and they went out the back door. He went through their routine, and he made her sit, shake, lay down, spin, roll over, and back up. She spoke for him, and quieted when he asked her to.

He threw a ball and made her wait. Then he told her to "Find it," and she ran after it. She searched and searched in the neighboring hay field, finally coming up with it and bringing it back to him. "Good girl," he said, giving her a treat. "Good."

He made her lie down again, and this time he threw the ball twice as far. "Find it," he told her. "Go."

Queen barked as she bounded out into the hay field. He'd been hiding other balls while she was out in the field, and he'd make her find a second one when she got back. One she hadn't seen where it had gone.

She barked out in the field, a joyous sound that made Brian smile. When she came back with the ball, Brian picked it up and said, "Find another one."

Queen cocked her head, and Brian said, "Find it."

She put her nose to the ground and started sniffing. She was such a smart dog, and it only took her about twenty seconds to find the ball he'd placed inside the rain gutter.

"Good girl." He grinned at her, and she barked as she dropped the ball. "Yes, I know." He chuckled as he bent to get it. "I'm tired, girl." He sank onto the steps. "Can we be done for tonight?"

Queen sat and panted, an earnest look on her face.

"Yeah, it's Seren," he said. "Come on. Let's go get something to eat." He went up the steps and into the house, where he opened the fridge and pulled out a container of pulled pork he'd gotten from Millie earlier in the week. He heated it and piled it on a roll with a slice of cheese before taking it to the couch and turning on the TV.

He waited for Seren to text him, but the minutes turned into an hour, and Brian ate and started to doze.

His phone did chime and bring him back to full consciousness, his heart tapping in a strange rhythm. But the text wasn't from Seren, and his pulse settled in the bottom of his boots.

Seth had texted, and Brian opened the message. *Good news! Jenna and I have been approved for adoption! We're meeting the birth mother tomorrow night, and we'd love your prayers.*

Brian's mouth curved into a smile, and he sent a message back to Seth. *Congrats! I'll definitely pray for you.*

Thanks, Seth sent, and Brian imagined he'd be really busy managing all the messages, so Brian didn't ask any other questions. He sure hoped this adoption went through, because Seth and Jenna had been this close before, and nothing had worked out yet.

Brian wanted to talk to Seren, but she hadn't texted him first all week. Still...Brian decided to bite the bullet and ask her if everything was okay between them. He typed out the message, not mincing words, and sent it.

Yes, Seren sent back. *Why?*

"Why?" Brian asked. Could she not feel the distance between them? He dialed Seren, hoping she'd answer. She obviously had her phone with her. Thankfully, she answered, because he wasn't sure what would've fractured if she hadn't.

"Hey," she said.

"Hey." He took a big breath. "What are you doing tonight?"

"Nothing. Sorrell and I are watching a sing-along."

"But you think we're okay."

"Yes," she said, her voice lowering. "I'm not sure why you think we're not."

"Because, Seren," he said. "I'm sitting home—alone—watching TV too. Couples who are okay want to spend time together on evenings they're free. Yet you're home with your sister, and I'm sitting here with my dog."

He forced himself to stop, because she deserved to say something to convince him that they really were okay.

She said nothing, and that only fueled Brian's frustration. "If you don't want to be with me," he said quietly. "Just say it."

"I'm not going to say that," she said. "I enjoy spending time with you."

"And yet we don't actually spend much time together."

"I'm just...dealing with some things right now."

"What kind of things?"

"Family things," Seren said. "It's a rough time of year for me, Brian."

Brian felt like a giant jerk, and he said, "I'm so sorry, Seren. Forgive me."

"It's okay," she said. "I guess we haven't been talking as much."

"I didn't know you were having a hard time. I wish you would've told me."

"I...don't know how to tell you things like that."

"You don't know how, or you don't want to?"

"I don't know," Seren said. "Maybe a little of both."

"Why don't you want to?"

"Because, Brian," she said. "I don't want you to think I'm weak."

"Seren," he said. "You're not weak, and I have literally never thought that about you. Everyone has rough times."

"Even you?"

"Uh, hello? I just texted you to ask if we were okay, because I wasn't sure. I've been doubting you and us and me for a week now. So yes, even me."

"Okay," she said. A lengthy pause followed, and then she asked, "What are you watching? Maybe I'll come sit with you."

"I don't even know," he said, looking at the screen. "But please come over. You can put on whatever you want." He knew he sounded desperate, but he wasn't sure he cared.

"All right," Seren said with a light laugh. "See you in a few minutes."

Brian lowered the phone, so glad he'd texted her. Maybe she was waiting for him to reach out to her each evening. If so, he needed to find out, because he wanted to feel needed and wanted too, and if he was the one always initiating everything, he simply felt like a creep going after a woman who clearly wasn't interested in him.

"Tell her when she gets here," he told himself, intending to do just that.

CHAPTER 18

Seren walked toward Brian's front door with confidence, and she knocked with plenty of power behind the motion.

"Yeah," Brian said from inside. "Just a sec." His voice sounded strange, because she could hear it from behind the door and from...over the roof. Almost like he had windows open in the back, so it echoed in the stillness of Chestnut Ranch.

A few seconds later, he opened the door, and all of Seren's confidence evaporated. He seemed totally different, and she scanned him from head to toe to try to figure out what it was. No cowboy hat. No cowboy boots.

This was the casual version of Brian Gray that dressed down after a busy day on the ranch. He wrapped his fingers over the top of the door and leaned into it, his smile curving his mouth in the most delicious way. "Hey."

"Hi." She fisted her fingers and stepped into the cabin.

She'd been here before, but not for long. Just to grab him on her way past to the homestead, where they'd spent hours painting, talking, laughing, and kissing. He'd invited her to dinner once, but their lives had been hectic, and it hadn't happened.

Since the job had completed a week or ten days ago, Seren had retreated back to Fox Hollow Ranch, where she needed the extra rest after working the overtime she'd had to put in to get a full week off to paint the homestead here.

She and Brian hadn't talked much; he was right about that. How did she tell him she was just tired?

"Thanks for coming," he said. "You want something to drink?"

"Sweet tea, if you have it."

"I have it." He took a few steps past the couch and arrived in the kitchen. Seren gazed around at this cabin he called home. She wondered why he lived here, in this box of a house that he didn't own. He had plenty of money—at least he'd said he did. Why did he choose to live this life? He could live in a mansion with people who did his cleaning and gardening for him, behind a gate where no one would bother him.

Seren noted that the cabin was clean and clutter-free. If Brian kicked off his boots somewhere, she couldn't see them. He turned from the fridge and put the pitcher of sweet tea on the dining table, because he had very little counter space. A fridge stood next to the entrance to the hallway, and Seren peered down that way.

It looked like there was only one bedroom here, with a

single bath as well. Next to the fridge, a microwave took up the available counter space, and then the cabinets turned, so he had a little countertop in the corner. Then the kitchen sink. Then a small patch of counter above the dishwasher, which immediately gave way to the stove. He had one more drawer-width spot of counter space at the end, and then the back door led outside.

The back door stood wide open, and Queen came inside in that moment, panting.

"There you are," Brian said, as he poured the sweet tea into two tall glasses. She hadn't even seen him get them down. The windows had no curtains, though they did have blinds. Everything was functional and placed in exactly the right spot to maximize the space.

He handed her one of the glasses, and Seren sipped the sweet tea. "Oh," she said. "This is good."

"You doubted me?" He moved over to the back door and closed it now that Queen was inside.

"Mm, you aren't Texan," she said, falling easily into teasing him.

He chuckled as he shook his head, and he reached up as if to adjust his cowboy hat, only to let his hand fall when he realized he wasn't wearing one. He took a drink of his sweet tea too.

"I just have the one couch," he said. "But it's fairly comfortable."

Queen drank loudly from her bowl while they moved the few steps into the front half of the cabin, which held the couch that faced the front wall. Brian had a TV mounted to that wall, with a shelf right below it that held DVDs and a couple of picture frames.

Seren didn't have to move closer to see them, because sitting on the couch put her in close enough proximity to make out his family with him and his brother as adults. Another woman stood next to who must be Tom, as well as two boys. Brian's nephews.

"Just your mom in that picture," she said.

"My parents are divorced," he said. "So yes, two family pictures are required."

"They don't get along?"

"That's why they got divorced," he said, quirking an eyebrow at her.

She gave him a small smile. "I just meant that sometimes couples that have been married a while are at least civil."

"They still wouldn't have a family picture together," he said.

"Okay." She took another drink. "And that's your dad?" She looked at the second picture, and this one was clearly old. Brian and Tom couldn't be out of high school yet, and she studied the younger version of the man she sat with on the couch.

"Yes, ma'am."

"How old are you in that photo?"

"Fifteen." He got up and collected the picture, bringing it back to the sofa. "My parents had just gotten divorced, and this was our first or second weekend with my dad." He looked at the picture, clearly seeing more than just the people smiling back at the camera.

"Did you live with your mom then?"

"They had joint custody," he said. "I'm the youngest, and I was fifteen. The judge let us choose." He handed her the picture. "Tom could drive, so my parents went in on a car for the two of us, and we went back and forth whenever and wherever we wanted. We just had to communicate to both of my parents."

"Wow." Seren looked at the two smiling boys in the picture, along with their father. "You look like you belong to them." They all had the same hair color, the same crinkly smiles, and the same square chin. "I guess you have your mother's eyes."

"She definitely made Tom and I a bit lighter than my dad." Brian relaxed into the couch and stretched his legs out, his feet up on the coffee table. Queen came over and jumped onto the couch, sending a few water droplets spraying. "Queen," Brian admonished and then grunted as the huge dog sat halfway on him, leaning her full weight against him. "Come on."

"She loves you," Seren said, watching the two of them. They were so cute, and Queen clearly adored Brian.

Brian smiled as he scrubbed behind Queen's ears. "There's not room for you, girl."

Seren got up and put the picture back on the shelf, then sat down farther from Brian so Queen would have room. The dog looked at her like, *so there. Thank you for moving, I suppose.* She really was a queen, and Seren shook her head as she smiled.

"You really can put on whatever you want," he said, handing her the remote control.

"I don't like that power," she said, refusing to take it. "You choose."

Brian kept the remote and pointed it at the TV. A moment later, the screen brightened. He flipped around the guide, and how he could read what was on before the screen advanced, Seren would never know. She didn't even think he was paying attention. "Seren?"

"Yeah?"

"At the risk of sounding needy, I've just got to say something."

Her stomach tightened, as did her fingers around the glass. "All right."

"I really like you—I think that's obvious. But I don't want to be the only one who calls and texts."

"I call you and text you."

"Always second," he murmured.

"What do you mean?"

"I mean you text me *back*. You call me *back*. You never call me first. You never text me first." He didn't look away from the TV, the guide just flipping and flipping. "It makes me feel like I'm chasing you. Like if I didn't text you, you wouldn't text me. Like you haven't this week."

"I've just been busy."

"Doing what?"

She really didn't like the somewhat aggressive tone of his voice. She pressed her lips together and stared at the screen too. "I had to pick up every extra shift this week, because I took off so much time to paint over here."

The guide finally stilled, and Seren felt the weight of Brian's gaze on the side of her face. "You did?"

"Yes. Yesterday, I worked sixteen hours. I had the dawn hike, as well as the evening dinner hike."

"Why didn't you tell me?"

"Honestly? I can barely think through the next hour. When I get home, I shower and put on loose clothes and fall onto the couch. If Sorrell didn't live with me, I wouldn't eat." She finally looked at him. "I'm sorry I haven't been texting you. I didn't even realize I was only responding and not initiating."

With Queen between them, she couldn't quite reach his hand, and he pushed the dog down and gestured for Seren to take her place. Seren did, sliding over on the couch and cuddling into Brian's side as he put his arm around her.

Queen jumped back onto the couch where she'd been, circled and huffed as she sat down.

"Oh, you're fine," Brian said.

Seren giggled into his chest. "You've spoiled her."

"Yeah," he said, not even bothering to deny it. "Listen, I... my first marriage failed because my wife wasn't nearly as interested in me as I was in her."

Seren tensed, but she didn't sit up to look at him. He moved through the guide much slower now, and she could practically hear the wheels turning in his head.

"I was only married for three months, because that's when I found out she'd been cheating on me. For a long time. Almost from the very beginning, and we dated for a year before we got engaged. Then another eight months."

Seren did the math quickly. Almost two years of his life he'd invested in his ex-wife, only to find out he was the only committed one.

"I'm not seeing anyone else," she said.

"Good," he said. "But maybe that'll help frame where I'm coming from. I'm not usually so...I don't know."

Emotional wasn't the right word, because Brian was fairly even. Way more even than Seren, who felt like she was manning a ship on stormy seas singlehandedly. The boat swayed from side to side constantly, dipped and rose with every wave the ship crested. Her mood was all over the place, she knew.

"You're not needy," she said. "I can see what you're saying now. I'll work on making sure you're not the only one initiating things between us."

"Thank you," he said with a sigh. This time, he put the remote in her hand. "You really should pick, because I think I'm going to fall asleep."

"That's what I want to do," she said.

"Then put something quiet on." He kneaded her closer and rested his head on hers. "Thanks for coming, Seren."

She found a movie she'd seen before—a romantic comedy that didn't have explosions or loud music—and put the remote on the couch between her and Queen. The silence in the cabin was as refreshing as the air conditioner, which worked really well.

Beside her, Brian's breathing evened and deepened, and Seren closed her eyes too, glad she'd come though she'd been a tad annoyed when he'd first called. Now, in the safety of his arms, feeling so comfortable in his cabin, and close to him both physically and emotionally, Seren fell asleep too.

* * *

A loud, pealing sound broke into Seren's amazing dream where she, Brian, and Queen had hiked to Chestnut Springs. It had been so hot, and Seren had gone into the water to cool down. Brian had followed, and he'd been kissing her when that terrible, shrill ringing interrupted her.

"That's a phone," Brian mumbled, moving beneath her.

Seren opened her eyes, her brain feeling soggy and slow. It was dark wherever she was—pure blackness surrounded her.

"It's not my phone," he said. "It's Sorrell, Seren." He bent and picked up the phone from the floor and handed it to her.

It felt like a brick in her hand, but she woke quickly now and swiped on the call. "Sorrell," she said.

"Do you know what time it is?" Sorrell asked. "Where are you? Are you okay? I'm about to call the police."

Behind her, Brian turned on the light in the kitchen, and it spilled over the back of the couch, making Seren squint. Her back hurt too, and she reached up to rub her forehead. "Uh, I fell asleep at Brian's."

"Did you now?"

"I'm fine, Sorrell," she said. "I'll be home in a few minutes."

"It's after midnight, Seren," Sorrell said.

"I'm sorry." She stood up, glad she didn't feel fuzzy anymore. Her mouth was a bit gluey, and she needed to use the bathroom. She could get a drink and take care of all of that at home. "I'll check in with you when I get home."

"I'll wait up."

"You don't need—"

"Then you can tell me what really happened," Sorrell said over her, and a moment later the call ended.

"So she's mad," Seren said, turning toward Brian. He stood at the table, looking at her. "Sorry, I have to go."

He nodded, and he looked absolutely dreamy fresh from sleep, bootless, and hatless. Despite her breath, she took the few steps to him and wrapped her hands around the back of his neck as she kissed him. He only used one hand, and it slid up her arm, across her shoulder, and into her hair.

"Take me to dinner tomorrow night?" she whispered, only an inch between them. "I'm off at six."

"I'll meet you in the parking lot like we used to," he whispered back. He kissed her again, and Seren checked for her phone and keys before ducking out his front door.

She didn't hear him lock it behind her, and she hurried back to Fox Hollow, where Sorrell had the porch light on, as well as every light inside the house too.

"Sorry," Seren said as soon as she walked through the front door. She did lock it behind her, and she switched off the lights for outside and the foyer before she hurried down the hall to the back of the house. Sorrell stood at the island in the kitchen, lasers in her eyes.

"We really did fall asleep."

"Mm hm." Sorrell nodded to the barstools, but Seren didn't have the energy.

"I have to work in the morning," she said.

"As do I," Sorrell said. "So imagine my surprise when I got up to check on the brisket and I realized you weren't here."

"I worked twelve hours today," Seren said. "Yesterday. Whenever. Trust me, I fell asleep on his couch." Seren glared at Sorrell. "Besides, I don't owe you an explanation."

"You don't?" Sorrell's eyebrows went up and she slapped the tongs on the counter. "That's rude. You could at least call if you're going to spend the night with your boyfriend."

"I didn't spend the night with my boyfriend," Seren practically growled. "And you know what's rude? You thinking I would." She shook her head. "I was raised the same way you were, Sorrell, and I think it's super unfair of you to assume the worst about me when nothing happened. And what did happen was really innocent." She started for the hallway. "And heaven forbid anyone make a mistake around the mighty Sorrell."

"What does that mean?" Her sister followed her, and Seren didn't want to fight with her.

"It means, Sorrell, that you're perfect, and I can never measure up." She opened the door to her bedroom, glad the fan was still in there. She'd need it to cool her temper. She turned back to her sister, who wore indignation on her face. "I don't want to argue with you. I'm sorry I didn't call or text. It was not my intention to stay for more than an hour or so, as I told you when I left the house earlier."

Sorrell softened, her eyes wide and round. "I'm sorry too."

Seren turned and stepped into Sorrell's arms. "I hope you

weren't worried, and I hope you don't really think I did anything wrong."

"I was worried," she said. "But it's okay." She held Seren tight, almost like she needed the pressure to keep them together. "I don't believe you did anything wrong."

"Thank you." Seren stepped back and gave Sorrell the biggest smile she could muster. "Good night."

"See you in the morning." Sorrell reached up and wiped her eyes, and Seren stepped into the bedroom, once again the one who *wasn't* crying.

She'd felt something sitting with Brian, though. As she changed into her pajamas, she told herself that not every emotion had to manifest itself in the form of tears. It didn't mean she was broken because she didn't cry the way Sorrell did.

She lay down in her cool bed, an image of Brian's face floating through her mind. She'd definitely felt something for him tonight. Something powerful. Something beyond just a crush. He'd said he really liked her, and Seren took a moment in the safe darkness of her bedroom to whisper, "I really like you too, Brian Gray."

Now she just had to figure out how to go from "really liking" a man to falling in love with him.

CHAPTER 19

Theo put his blinker on and slowed down, getting ready to turn right. He did, the tires slipping a bit as he went from asphalt to dirt. In front of him, a tall, arched sign spanned over the two-lane road.

The Singer Ranch.

His heart beat wildly in his chest, but he kept the truck moving. Immediately, he could tell this ranch was much more commercial than Fox Hollow. Not a single blade of grass was overgrown, and every fence pole stood exactly straight.

They were a much bigger operation than Fox Hollow, and Theo caught sight of a row of cabins on another road to his right. Windmills stood guard in these front fields, and the homestead sprawled on the left side, the grass emerald green surrounding it.

It had four garages, and a couple more trucks parked in the long driveway. The trees were mature and cast shade over the house and yard, and everything looked straight out of a magazine.

Theo continued past the turn-off for the house, his goal another building on the ranch coming up on the right. The administration building. Sarena ran the affairs of Fox Hollow from her house or an office in the barn. But this ranch had a foreman, who worked in an office full-time, in a building dedicated to running the ranch.

Theo parked in front of the building, which was a double-wide trailer that looked like it had just been bleached. He grabbed the folder with his résumé and letters of recommendation before heading inside.

Air conditioning kept the space cool, and he glanced right and then left, where he found a series of three desks stretching toward the far wall.

"You must be Theo," the woman at the closest desk said. "C'mon in, sugar."

Theo was already in, but he stepped in her direction, reaching up to tip his hat. "I am Theo," he said. "Theodore Lange." He extended his hand for her to shake. "Are you Courtney?"

"Yes, sir," she drawled. "You've got paperwork?"

"Yes, ma'am." He handed her the folder, and she perched on the edge of her desk as she flipped through it.

"Looks good," she said only ten seconds later. No way she could've read it that fast. "Winn will be in in a minute. You can go sit at his desk. He's at the back."

"Thank you." Theo went that way, feeling her eyes on

every inch of his body. He didn't like it, but he just kept his head down and sat at the desk in the corner of the building.

True to her word, the door opened a few minutes later, and a booming voice filled the trailer with, "Court, I need you to take care of the helicopter."

Theo turned to see a bear of a man standing just inside the door. He nodded to Courtney, who took something from him and said, "Yes, sir. Your interview is here. Theo Lange. Level one."

Winn's eyes moved to his desk, and Theo stood up. "Ah, yes." Winn grinned, but he looked more like a wolf than a man as he came toward Theo. "Theo Lange. From Fox Hollow, right?"

"I'm there now, yes," Theo said. "Before that I was at—"

"Lantern Ridge." Winn shook his hand and gestured for Theo to sit down again. He went around the desk and sat with a loud groan. "So, Theo, why'd you go from a mid-size ranch to a speck operation?"

"Just needed a change," Theo said. "But I've been at Fox Hollow for a while now, and I think I'm ready for another change."

"Six years at Fox Hollow, I believe," Winn said, though he wasn't looking at a single piece of paper.

"Seven, actually," Theo said. "But yes, a while."

"No complaints there?"

Theo thought of Sorrell, her beautiful face moving through his mind at a million miles an hour. He shook his head. "Mm, no sir."

"But they didn't write you a letter."

Theo wanted to ask him how he'd known that. Theo had been instructed to bring his letters of recommendation to the interview, and the folder still sat on Courtney's desk. Maybe she'd texted him. "No," he said. "Sarena Adams would, if I asked her. But I haven't told her I'm looking for a new position at a new ranch."

"Why's that?" Winn cocked his head and studied Theo. "You know we're looking to fill our position immediately. You won't give them two weeks' notice?"

"I intend to," Theo said. "I didn't realize this job wouldn't allow me to tie up loose ends." He'd waited a month for them to even respond to his application. Then he'd had a phone call with Courtney, and she'd asked him all of these questions already, as well as how long he'd been working ranches in Texas, if he had any special animal training, and if he knew how to use all the big ranch equipment. He'd been able to answer in the affirmative for everything except the helicopter.

Just the fact that The Singer Ranch was so big it required a helicopter was well outside Theo's realm of ranching.

"It will," Winn said.

"Great," Theo said. "If I get the job, I'll need two weeks before I can move and start." He swallowed just thinking about that conversation with Sarena. At the same time, he knew it wasn't Sarena he'd have to answer to, but Sorrell.

She'd cry, and Theo would feel like a real jerk. He wouldn't be able to explain. He didn't want her to think she was the reason he was leaving the ranch, though she was. She'd cry every day if she knew that, and there was no point in hurting her for no reason.

Winn smiled at him. "You have medication training?"

"Yes, sir."

"How many cows did you deliver last year?"

Theo took a deep breath and blew it out. "Sarena and I handle all the birthing. We had ninety-four births last year."

"How many assisted?"

"Twenty-seven," he said instantly. "I handle all of those."

Winn nodded, his eyes never leaving Theo's. "There's a place for you here, son, if you want it."

"I do," Theo said before he could second-guess everything he'd been feeling the past few months.

"Great." Winn stood up. "I'll let Court know, and she'll handle all the hiring paperwork, as well as your cabin assignment. We double up out here."

"That's fine," Theo said, though he could feel his freedom and privacy dry up on the spot. He stood up and shook Winn's hand.

"Two weeks."

"Two weeks," Theo repeated, the first hint of excitement moving through him now. He nodded to Winn, turned, and left the building. Then the ranch. "Holy cow," he muttered to himself as he passed under the arch. "You just got a job at The Singer Ranch."

He laughed then, the sound bright and full, something Theo hadn't felt coursing in his bloodstream for a long time. As he quieted, he started thinking about how he would tell Sarena that he was leaving the ranch where he'd worked for the past seven years in just two weeks.

He had almost a forty-five minute drive, and he could have

a speech ready by the time he got back to Fox Hollow. He picked up his phone and dialed Sarena, though, or else he might chicken out and not tell her until morning.

"Hey," Sarena said. "What's up?"

"I need to meet with you when I get back," Theo said.

"All right." She seemed distracted, and she definitely wasn't worried. "When's that?"

"An hour," Theo said, buying himself a few extra minutes. For what, he didn't know. "In the barn office?"

"Sure," she said. "Then we need to get out to the equipment shed and figure out what the heck is wrong with that baler."

"Stephen hasn't figured it out yet?"

"Not yet," she said with a sigh. "He cut himself this morning, and Darren thought it was bad enough to take him to the hospital. They've been gone for a while."

"So you're behind."

"Beyond," she said. "I've deemed it Sunday essentials."

Theo nodded. "Okay, I'll help get everything done when I get back."

"Great, see you soon."

The call ended, and Theo swallowed, finding his throat so dry. She'd definitely been too busy or too distracted to ask him where he'd gone. He'd told her he had "an appointment," and she hadn't questioned him further.

"Hey, you didn't lie," he muttered to himself as he drove.

The hour flew by, and before he knew it, Theo had arrived back at Fox Hollow and stood in Sarena's office. She wasn't there yet, and he just stared out the window where the sunlight poured in.

Her desk was messy, filled with papers and receipts. Even the label from a bag of feed loitered there. She'd probably ripped it off so she could reorder easily, and Theo experienced a powerful moment of doubt.

How could he leave this ranch? These sisters? He'd been working here for a long time, and he loved them. He knew they loved him.

Not Sorrell, he thought, and that strengthened his resolve. If nothing was going to happen there, it was simply time to move on.

"Hey," Sarena said, breaking him out of his thoughts. She sat behind the desk. "Sitting is probably a bad idea. I might never get up again." She laughed and smiled at him. "What's up, Theo? Sit down."

He shook his head, his jaw so tight. "Sarena, I don't know how to say this."

"What's going on?" She rose too, pressing her palms into the desk and leaning into them.

He swallowed, his mind flying through the decisions he'd made. It felt like seven years' worth of memories were regurgitating themselves through his brain in that single moment. He took a breath and said, "I've taken another job at another ranch. I'll be leaving Fox Hollow in two weeks."

Sarena's eyes widened, and she too pulled in a breath. Hers was much sharper and much louder, though. "You're quitting?"

"Yes," he said.

"Theo." She rounded the desk, panic in her expression now. "Why? Is it money? I can pay you more."

He wanted to close his eyes and disappear. He blinked, but the ground didn't open up and swallow him whole. "It's not money." If there was one thing Theo had plenty of, it was money. "I just need a change."

Sarena came to stand in front of him, her eyes searching his face. He looked over her shoulder, through all that cheery sunlight and out the window.

"It's Sorrell."

"I just need a change," Theo said again.

"Have you told her?"

He dropped his gaze to meet Sarena's. "No."

"She's going to be crushed."

"Is she?"

"Theo," Sarena chastised him. "Of course she is."

"I don't think so," he said, his neck tightening. "Besides, I don't have to tell her. I only have to clear it with you. You own the ranch."

"If you want to quit, Theo, you're going to have to tell Sorrell yourself."

"Is that the requirement?"

"Yes," Sarena said as if just seizing onto the idea. "That's the requirement."

"Okay." He turned to leave the office. He'd come this far. He could go a little further. He had to. He couldn't keep living and working here, with Sorrell so close and yet completely out of his reach. It was torture to his soul, and Theo had had enough.

He'd made it halfway down the aisle toward the exit when Sarena called, "Theo?"

He paused and turned back to her. She joined him in the hall, her eyes filled with all kinds of new emotions. Theo detected fear, worry, doubt, resignation, and more.

"You're really quitting." She wasn't asking this time.

"Yes," he said. "I'm real sorry, Sarena. I know it doesn't give you much time. There's a lot of cowboys that would love to come work here. I don't think you'll have a problem finding one."

"Just tell me it's not because of me, or because Fox Hollow is small."

"Sarena." Theo sighed and shook his head. He wanted to hug her and reassure her, so he did just that. He gathered her into his arms and said, "You're the best boss I've ever had, and I've loved working a small ranch. It's neither of those things."

She held him tight, and Theo really was going to miss her. He had spoken absolutely true. He'd loved his time here, but even good things ended, and it was time to find something else to love. *Someone* else.

"So it's Sorrell," she whispered.

"Yes," Theo whispered back, thinking if he didn't say it too loudly, it wouldn't be true. "It's Sorrell."

Sarena stepped back and wiped her eyes. "I'm really going to miss you, Theo." She raised her chin, because she was strong and determined, and he knew she could run this ranch alone and be just fine.

"I'm going to miss you too, Sarena." He faced the exit

again. "Can you say a prayer for me? I think I'm going to need it to talk to Sorrell."

He walked away, glad when Sarena called, "I'm starting now, Theo. Good luck."

As he went outside and basked in the heat and sunshine, he murmured, "Dear Lord, I need more than luck to make it through this next conversation."

Chapter 20

Sorrell looked over to the back door when it opened. Her pulse spiked when Theo walked in, and she almost leapt to her feet. She coached herself to move slowly, because she'd had a busy day at work and her feet hurt.

So much so, that she groaned when she stood. "Hey," she said, never too tired to give him a smile.

"Hey." Theo didn't return the smile, but that wasn't that unusual.

"You hungry?"

"No." He turned toward her as she passed him, moving into the kitchen. "Sorrell."

She paused, because she'd literally never heard Theo say he wasn't hungry. She continued around the island anyway, her goal the fridge. She didn't quite make it, because the seriousness of his tone had registered with her. "What's wrong?"

Theo's jaw clenched, and that made Sorrell's heart do the same. "I need to ask you something."

Her stomach flipped now too, because he'd said that to her before. He was finally going to ask her out again, and Sorrell could practically taste the *yes* on the back of her tongue. She grinned at him, a new energy prancing through her despite her terrible, long day at work. "Go on, then."

He ducked his head, and he was *so adorable*. "After I move out, will you still invite me to Thanksgiving dinner?" He lifted his eyes to hers again. "You always make the best mashed potatoes."

"Sure," she said, a squeal halfway out of her mouth when her brain sounded a siren. The world fuzzed in front of her. "Wait. What?"

"I'm moving away," he said, his words not taking on any meaning inside Sorrell's mind. "I took a new job at a different ranch."

The air left her lungs, and Sorrell felt like she couldn't get another breath. To make matters worse, it felt like someone had pushed her down and was now jumping on her chest to make sure every last ounce of air left her body.

"I'm sorry things didn't work out between us," Theo said. "And I hope you understand that this has nothing to do with you. It's just time for me to move on."

"Move on," she echoed, because her brain couldn't hold on to more than two words at the moment.

"Yes." Theo came toward her, and she smelled the leather that always accompanied him. The musky cologne. The maleness of his skin. He reached toward her as if he'd touch her with those hands, his skin against hers.

He hesitated and stopped. "I just have a couple of weeks

left here with you sisters. Will you throw me a big going-away party?" He smiled at her then, and the gesture was absolutely devastating in more ways than one.

He was so handsome that Sorrell's nerves buzzed at her to be excited that he was smiling in her direction.

Going-away party streamed through her mind, only leaving room for numbness. The buzzing and the numbness warred inside her, and Sorrell couldn't move.

"You don't have to," he said, inching closer to her. He seemed to be fighting a battle too, and he finally lifted his hand and curled his fingers around the back of her neck. He leaned down and pressed his lips to her forehead, and Sorrell closed her eyes, this single moment in time pure bliss.

"I have to go, Sorrell," he whispered, and she wasn't sure if he meant right now or if he meant in the grand scheme of things. "I'll miss you the most."

With that, he dropped his hand, stepped away, and walked out the back door. Sorrell stared at it as it swung closed, the resulting clunk as it closed shocking her system back into a functioning state.

She burst into tears right there in the kitchen, great racking sobs wrenching their way through her chest. Each breath burned. Each moment was agony.

Theo was leaving the ranch. He hadn't come here to ask her to dinner, but to say good-bye. She fled down the hall to her bedroom, as this had just become the third worst day of her life, behind the deaths of her parents.

* * *

"She's in here," Sarena said sometime later. Sorrell didn't know how much later. The sun hadn't set yet, but it was August, and she sometimes felt like she lived in Alaska during August, when the sun never seemed to go down.

Her older sister entered the bedroom, pure sympathy on her face. She already knew, which made sense, as she was Theo's boss.

Her younger sister came in too, and she was dressed in a cute pair of skinny black pants which only showed off how trim and tight Seren was. She also wore a bright blue blouse and strappy sandals, which meant she'd had a date with Brian.

Sorrell had ruined that too.

A fresh wave of tears pressed behind her eyes, and she held them back as long as she could. When Sarena sat on the bed and hugged her, Sorrell lost the fight with her emotions.

"We brought reinforcements," Seren said, joining everyone on the bed. "I have the coconut tres leches cupcake in the fridge for you, Sorrell, and I brought in the molten chocolate lava cake for right now."

"I haven't had dinner," Sorrell said through her tears, as if that mattered.

"Darren brought your favorite Chinese," Sarena said. "It's in the kitchen, waiting for you too."

"You can eat dessert first for once," Seren said, her face miraculously dry. Sorrell really wished she could be more like her sisters. She craved Sarena's strength and determination, and she'd love to be able to stuff away her feelings as if they didn't exist the way Seren did.

As it was, she didn't know how to do the things either of

them did. She took the spoon Sarena handed her, and the plate with the perfectly petite lava cake on it, her admiration of it something that gave her pause.

She loved cooking and baking and making pretty plates like this. She liked entertaining, and she was very good at putting events together, making the perfect menu, and filling the farmhouse with laughter and the scent of something brown and baked.

Nothing she'd done had kept Theo here.

She took her first bite of lava cake, the gooey dessert exactly what a perfect lava cake should be. "Sweet Tooth Fairy?" she asked.

"Yes," Seren said.

"Is that where you went with Brian tonight?" Sorrell looked up, because Seren wasn't great at keeping the truth out of her eyes.

She didn't even try this time. "Yes," she said, shooting a look at Sarena. "But it's fine. We were finishing up."

Sorrell heard the lie but didn't call Seren on it. Misery filled her stomach with every bite of the sweet treat she took. She knew Seren hadn't seen much of Brian in the past week or so, and that he'd been upset when he'd called last night. They hadn't gone out in weeks, and now Sorrell was supposed to believe that they'd been wrapping up their date long before the sun set?

She shook her head, her eyes burning again.

"He said it has nothing to do with you," Sarena said.

Sorrell pulled in a hard breath and glared at her sister. "He's a liar. And so are you."

"Sorry," Sarena said, picking at the blanket. "I just don't want you to blame yourself."

"Sorrell, just go tell him how you feel," Seren said, a note of desperation in her voice. "He'll stay if you just march down there and say, 'Look, I really like you, and I want to go to dinner with you.'" She exchanged another glance with Sarena, and surprisingly, Seren looked distressed, like she might cry. She was definitely emotional. "Ask him out and ask him to stay."

The idea was intriguing—and Sorrell knew she'd never do it.

I'll miss you the most.

She shook her head. While he had said he'd miss her, he'd also said he had to go. She handed the plate back to Sarena. "I'm fine."

"You are not fine." Sarena stood up and reached for Sorrell. "Come eat. Maybe you'll feel better."

Sorrell put her hand in her sister's, because Sarena had always been there for her. Always one step ahead, but always there. Sorrell had honestly dated the most out of any of them, and she'd never thought her sisters would leave the farmhouse. She'd never considered that they'd leave her.

She'd always thought she'd leave them.

Sarena was married now, with a baby on the way. She was a thousand steps ahead of Sorrell, and Sorrell couldn't remember a time she'd been this miserable.

Even Seren had a boyfriend, and it sure seemed like it was getting serious. Sorrell would be left behind, at the farmhouse, and she had no idea what the future looked like for her without her sisters.

The three of them—it had always been the three of them —sat down to dinner together, and Sarena and Seren started brainstorming ways to get Theo to stay. When Sorrell had taken a dozen bites—she knew Sarena would be counting— she pushed her plate away and looked at them.

"He's going," she said. "We shouldn't be talking about how to get him to stay. We should be talking about what we're going to do about hiring another cowboy."

"I've already put it on the job board," Sarena said, glancing around. "I put up two jobs, actually." She swallowed, her expression full of fear. "I'm going to have a baby, you know. Can't work the ranch quite the same way anymore."

"Can we afford two full-time cowboys?" Seren asked.

"Yes," Sarena said. "The ranch does really well for its size. We'll be fine."

"Oh, okay."

Sorrell stared at the cashew chicken on her plate, her mind wandering as her sisters continued to talk around her. In her mind, she saw herself walking out to Theo's cabin. She knocked on the door and begged him not to go. She told him she liked him so much, and she asked him if he'd like to go to dinner with her.

In her mind, he grinned and lifted her right off her feet. He said yes in a loud voice, and then he kissed her before they even left the porch.

She closed her eyes, the fantasy actually painful. Why

would her brain conjure up such a thing? Wasn't she tortured enough?

"I think we lost her," Seren said. "Sorrell?"

"Yes." She blinked her way out of the deep, dark place where she was currently hiding. "What?"

"You're not going to go talk to him, are you?" Sarena asked.

Sorrell shook her head and stood up. "I'm going to bed." She sniffled as she left the kitchen, and she'd changed out of her slacks and blouse and into her pajamas when her sisters both entered her room again.

The three of them lay down in her bed, the other two sandwiching Sorrell between them. "Go on, now," Seren whispered. "Just cry it all out, Sorrell." She smoothed her hair off her forehead, and Sorrell looked into her younger sister's eyes. Seren wore kindness there, and she smiled a little. "It's going to be okay."

"I don't see how," Sorrell whispered.

"Sometimes we can't," Sarena said from behind. "But God knows how it works out."

The three of them had piled into one bed the day their mother had died too, and Sorrell had thought she wouldn't survive that torment. Somehow, she had. Somehow, the sun still rose each day. Somehow, God did take the reins and heal hearts.

Sorrell physically felt every wall she'd ever had the strength to build come crumbling down, and she did just what Seren had given her permission to do—she cried it all out.

Chapter 21

Brian's shoulders ached, but he wasn't making two trips to haul the dog food out into the run. He hefted the buckets, a grunt coming from his mouth, and got moving. This was the fourth day of walking the buckets out to the dogs who didn't live in an enclosure, the "lifers" as Seth liked to call them. The dogs who weren't up for adoption, and wouldn't go up for adoption. They had settled into life with Queen as their alpha, and Brian wasn't breaking up nearly as many fights anymore.

The ATV he usually used had been in the equipment shed with an as still undiagnosed problem. All he knew was that he'd driven the buckets out to feed the dogs a few days ago, finished the job, and then the ATV wouldn't start. He'd pushed it back through hundred-degree temperatures, sweating buckets, and falling behind on the job.

Griffin had been working on it, but he had plenty of regular chores around the ranch too, and he hadn't dedicated much time to finding the problem. He'd just told Seth yesterday to call a real mechanic, and that left Brian hauling the food by hand.

A dog growled to his right, but Brian just looked at the pitbull there. Roxy didn't like anyone, and Brian didn't take it personally. It was also why she lived out here in the run. He encountered several other dogs along the way, and they came over to him and trotted alongside him, the dust lifting into the air as they all walked.

He finally reached the group of trees where the dogs lived. Most of them, at least. A grouping of ten doghouses had been built out here, and Brian had done at least half of them himself. He grabbed the rake, and cleared the area around the houses, then poured the food into the bowls.

The dogs had to have fresh water four times a day in heat like this, and Brian started back to the nearest enclosure, which was a quarter-mile from this outer living area.

"Go on," he said to Samson, a quick, medium-sized mutt who had a nice room in enclosure four. "This isn't for you." He passed the black and white dog. "Come on, Sam. Come with me."

The dog did what he said, and they walked back to the enclosure together. He put out fresh water for Samson, filled the two buckets with cold water from the pump, and took a deep breath in.

"Two more trips." He could do this. The dog operation on the ranch was still new, and Seth was still getting all the pieces together. He'd ordered a watering system for the dogs, but the construction of it was slow. Until then, Brian would do what he had to in order to take care of the dogs.

He made the first trip without incident. As he drew closer to the houses and trees for the last time that afternoon—Rex would do this evening's watering—Brian heard snarling.

A bark sounded, and then a flurry of them. He hurried to set the buckets down, trying to look at them and find the problem in front of him at the same time. Some of the water he'd painstakingly carried splashed out, filling him with frustration.

He told himself to leave it and find the dog fight. If he didn't, he could find himself with another hour of work—this time, digging a hole for a dead dog.

"Hey," he said, finding the scuffle. Surprisingly, it was George and Yeti. He supposed Yeti wasn't all that surprising, as the bulldog had a big chip on his shoulder, and he was ultra-possessive about unpredictable things. George was a mostly sweet Akita who normally didn't have a problem with any of the other dogs.

Brian yipped as loudly as he could as he ran toward the dogs. "Stop it! Enough. Enough." He wished he'd had a moment to run over to the bowls to grab the rake. He didn't think his hands would survive against Yeti's snapping teeth.

"George, go," Brian said, pointing behind him. Thankfully, the Akita knew those two words, and he backed up enough that Brian could get between him and Yeti. "Shh." He held out one hand, palm down, and kept making the obnoxious shushing noise mixed with the beginning of the word *church* until Yeti lay down.

"Stay," he told the dog. He didn't look away from it, though a line of sweat ran right along the corner of his left eye. "Calm." He shushed the dog again, and Yeti's eyelids started to drift halfway closed. His tongue lolled out of his mouth, and Brian started to relax.

"Go on," he told the other dogs. He shuffled right quickly when Finny tried to come over to Yeti. "Nope. Go, Finny." He took his time, because he wanted Yeti in a completely calm state of mind, and he needed the dog to trust him. By "protecting" Yeti from Finny, perhaps Yeti would continue to obey Brian.

His phone rang, but he ignored it, taking several long minutes before he even lowered his hand. "All right," he said. "Come on."

Yeti lumbered to his feet, taking one slow step at a time as he came toward Brian. Brian crouched down and said, "Come on, Yeti. You can do it."

The dog panted heavily as he came to Brian, and Brian knew exactly how he felt. "It's hot, ain't it?" He held out his hand and let Yeti smell it and then rub his head against it. "That's right. Now, come on. You can't be arguing with the other dogs over nothin', okay?" He used both hands to scrub behind Yeti's ears. "Okay. Now we've got more water to deliver."

He straightened, his back protesting. His shoulders and arms did too. "Almost done," he told himself. He made it back to the buckets, and because he was so close, he only picked up one. He could go this far again.

His phone rang again, but Brian didn't even take it from

his pocket. After he got the dogs watered. He made the trips required, noting how most of the dogs out here had their little packs or favorite places. Some lay alone at the base of trees, and others sat in their houses. Some had a group of two or three they lay by, and some only came in to eat and drink, and then they headed back out into the run.

Brian hauled the empty buckets back to the enclosure, noting how golden the sun had become in the sky. "Shoot," he muttered, stepping into the air conditioned enclosure. He pulled his phone out and looked at it, Seren's name swirling on the screen.

He groaned as everything spun, and he seriously didn't have time for this right now. He was already late finishing his work, and the one night—the *one night*—he'd managed to get a date with Seren, he wasn't going to make it.

Leaning against the sink, he pressed his eyes closed and took a deep breath. Then another. Another. Finally, his heartbeat started to relax, and the swirling, multi-colored lights flashing through his vision slowed and stopped.

"Okay," he said with a sigh. He opened his eyes and tapped to dial Seren back. She didn't answer, and Brian's irritation grew and multiplied until he felt like it was suffocating him.

His phone rang again, and he quickly swiped on the call from Seren. "Hey," she said, and she didn't sound any happier than he felt. "Listen, I have to cancel tonight."

"You do?" Brian had thought she was going to ask him where he was, not cancel. "You've canceled three times now."

"I just..." She exhaled heavily and offered no other explanation.

Brian didn't need one. He knew what was going on at Fox Hollow Ranch. Theo was moving to The Singer Ranch in a few days, and Sorrell was falling apart. Brian didn't see why he and Seren should have to do the same thing, but he hadn't found a way to tell Seren she had a right to be happy even if Sorrell wasn't.

"It's fine," Brian said, though he didn't feel fine. He wanted to see his girlfriend. He'd had a terrible day, and everything hurt, and lounging on the couch alone was the last thing he wanted to do that evening.

"It's not fine," Seren said.

"No," Brian said. "I'm not fine." He stormed out of the enclosure, remembered he had to mark the clipboard to communicate with the others, and went back. "I have to go." He hung up, his anger morphing from his frustration.

He yanked the clipboard from the wall inside the door, marked that he'd fed and watered the dogs at six-twelve, and left again.

His phone rang again, and he swiped on the call from Seren but didn't say anything.

"This isn't a barrel of fun for me either," she said, no *hello*. No *I'm sorry*. No *I wish things could be different*.

Brian wished so many things could be different.

He got behind the wheel of his truck, the interior so hot he couldn't get a proper breath. "I just have one question, Seren."

"Fine," she bit out.

Brian started the car, the words forming into sentences in his mind. He got the air conditioning blowing and the windows down so he didn't suffocate in the meantime. "Will you ever pick me over her?"

"Over who?" she asked, but she knew who. Brian didn't need to specify.

"Brian," she said, plenty of frustration in her voice too.

"I understand family," he said, backing away from the enclosure too fast. "I really do, Seren. But I don't want to be Sorrell's second fiddle. That might make me selfish. A terrible man. I don't know. I know she's going through a hard time. I don't wish her any ill will. I just..." He paused as he turned and put the truck in drive. "I feel like you're always going to put me second."

The fact that she didn't immediately contradict him told Brian everything he needed to know. "I have to go, Seren." He hung up on her again, a twinge of regret stinging behind his heart.

His phone rang almost immediately, as he hadn't even tossed it to the seat in disgust yet. Seren. Again.

"Might as well answer it," he muttered, sliding on the call. "Yeah?"

"If you hang up on me one more time...that is so rude."

"There's nothing else for me to say," he said, his patience already gone. "And I'd really rather not say something I'll regret later, so trust me, hanging up is better."

"Yeah? Let's see how you like it then."

"Seren—" The line went dead.

Brian gripped the phone with as much strength as he had in his hands. The open window was looking like a mighty fine place to chuck his phone. Instead, he tossed it on the seat next to him, rolled up the windows, and went home.

Inside the cabin, he stopped and looked around. The only thing he liked about this place in that moment was that it was cool. He hated the curtain-less windows. The tiny kitchen. The pathetic shelf with two family photos.

Brian felt like yelling until his throat hurt. He wanted to pick up anything and everything and throw it against the wall. Maybe if something shattered into a million pieces, he wouldn't have to feel like it was his heart breaking all over again.

"Why do I always pick the women who don't want me?"

Queen chose that moment to come into the house through the back door, and she perked up when she saw Brian. She trotted over to him, and he fell to his knees and buried his face in her scruff. "At least I have you, Queen," he whispered, though surely she didn't know what he meant.

He loved her, but having a dog was definitely not the same as having Seren in his life. "Okay, I can't kneel here. It hurts."

Everything hurt, and he stopped in the kitchen for a few painkillers before he went down the hall to shower.

He didn't feel any better once he was clean, and as he pulled out a microwave meal that would be a dinner of beef stew and mashed potatoes in four minutes, he realized something big.

"Theo has the right idea," he said aloud, a hint of awe in his voice. "I need a fresh start. Somewhere an hour away—or more. Somewhere where I won't have to think about how easy it would be to show up on the front steps of that blasted farmhouse, begging Seren to take me back."

He wasn't going to do that again. He'd done it twice already, and he deserved to hold onto some pride.

With the microwave whirring, Brian got out his laptop, which he hardly ever used. It was charged, though, and it connected him to the Internet before the beef stew finished. Now he just needed to find a new job.

CHAPTER 22

Seren couldn't sleep after the horrible phone calls with Brian, as well as another night of misery with Sorrell. She'd taken the first two days of this week off work, but thankfully, she had meetings for the upcoming blind bachelor auction the city was doing the weekend after Thanksgiving, and she had to get up, put her brave face on, and go to work.

Seren hated leaving her during the day, but she had a job too. "Why can't you leave her at night then, to go out with Brian?"

She could, and she knew it. Sorrell hadn't asked her to stay, though it was implied. She'd made huge dinners every night since learning about Theo's imminent departure from the ranch, and Sarena and Darren had come almost every evening.

They hadn't come last night, and Seren didn't have the heart to leave her sister home alone after she'd been gone all day already. She hadn't realized Brian would react so negatively.

"He just had a bad day," she told herself as she drove to town. She was actually going in the wrong direction, but she wanted to get his favorite coffee and be on his doorstep before he left to work the ranch. To do that, she had to be there almost before the sun rose, so it was probably a good thing she couldn't sleep.

Half an hour later, with his favorite coffee—laced with chocolate and cinnamon—she pulled up to his cabin. His truck still sat out front, so her hopes that he hadn't left yet remained high. She gathered her courage and walked across his lawn, up the steps, and to the front door.

"Brian?" she asked against the seam where the door met the jamb. She knocked lightly and waited a few seconds. "It's Seren."

She heard bootsteps coming, and she backed up just as he pulled open the door. He simply gawked at her, and she employed all of her energy to hold his gaze. "I brought you some coffee," she said, though the scent of it wafted from his house.

"Seren," he said, his voice made of air. He took the coffee and then took her into his arms. "It's so good to see you."

Seren melted into his touch, glad she'd been able to think of something to help him. Thinking of others and what she could do for them was something that her non-emotional side often prevented her from doing. She thought about other people; she just didn't know how to relate to them.

"Can we try for dinner tonight?" she asked. "I've already

texted Sarena, and she said she'll come down to the house tonight."

"I can't tonight," he said, backing up and looking over her shoulder. "Tomorrow?"

"That should work," she said, all of her plans changing in that one moment. "What are you doing tonight?"

"Ranch meeting," he said, his eyes only meeting hers for a moment.

"Oh." Seren frowned, because she thought they did those during the day. The Johnson brothers were all married, some of them with families. "Okay." She reached up and put her hand on the side of his face. "I'm sorry for hanging up on you. I was angry, and it's been a trying couple of weeks."

"That it has." He leaned into her palm. "I'm sorry I hung up on you too."

"We're okay?"

"Yeah," he said, his voice taking on a false quality that made Seren's skin prickle. "We're okay. I'll call you tonight after my meeting?"

"Sure," she said, smiling at him.

"Thank you for the coffee." He lifted it to his lips and sipped, a smile finally brightening his face and bringing out the Brian she knew.

In that moment, she realized what had just happened. He lifted his hand in a good-bye wave, and she did the same, almost stumbling in her haste to leave his porch and get back to the safety of her car.

"He lied to me," she whispered as she put the key in the ignition. Her stomach tightened, and her chest felt like a giant had laid down on it for a long winter's nap. She couldn't get a decent breath, and a strong feeling of betrayal moved through her.

She threw an angry look toward his front door, but he'd already closed it and was nowhere in sight. "Ranch meeting," she muttered. "Where are you really going to be tonight, Brian?"

Seren worked through the day. When she arrived back on the ranch, Sorrell's car wasn't in front of the farmhouse. It really would've been a perfect night for a date with Brian. Her mind revved up again, and she began to stew on him. She'd only gone a few minutes at a time that day where she wasn't thinking about him, and pure exhaustion filled her.

She had half a mind to drive over to Chestnut Ranch and knock on Russ's door. If he was there, she'd know there was no ranch meeting. In her heart of hearts, she already knew. Having proof would only make her feel worse, not better.

Sorrell had been cooking so much that the fridge was full of food, and Seren stood in front of it, nothing appetizing in view. She closed the fridge and sighed. Though it had only been twenty-four hours since the disastrous phone calls, and only twelve since Brian had told her they were okay, Seren felt like everything had shifted.

They stood on new ground now, and she didn't know how to traverse it. There were hills and valleys she didn't understand, and she knew everything about hiking and the best way up a mountain. This mountain felt impossible to climb.

An hour passed, and Sorrell returned home from work. "There you are," Seren said. "I was beginning to worry."

"Just a long day," Sorrell said, her voice nearly a monotone as she went right past where Seren sat in the living room and down the hall. She didn't come back either, and Seren alternated between staring at the clock and then the TV.

Time moved so slowly; darkness fell; she went down the hall to her bedroom too.

Brian hadn't called.

The next day, the sun rose, and with it, Seren did as well. Sorrell got off to work, leaving Seren standing in the kitchen, wondering if this was how her relationship with Brian died— in silence, with a lie bulging between them.

Probably more than one lie, she thought. He'd lied about the ranch meeting. He'd lied when he'd said he'd call her afterward. He'd lied when he said they were okay.

They obviously weren't okay.

She didn't take him coffee. She led groups up to the top of Enchantment Rock, counting down the days until school would start again and all she'd have left to deal with were the tourists. The park would still be busy, as it was one of the premier locations in the Texas Hill Country. Seren might actually get a day off, or she might be able to eat her lunch without having to talk and walk as she did.

She went home that afternoon, actually turning off her phone and resetting it to make sure she hadn't missed any of

Brian's calls or texts. They were supposed to go out that night, and he always made the plans.

He doesn't want to always be the one to reach out, she reminded herself, and as soon as she could do so safely, she pulled off the road and texted him. *Hey, are we still on for dinner tonight? Want to pick me up at six? I'm headed home now.*

She stared at the words, imagining them to be from another woman who actually felt cheery and excited to see her boyfriend. In reality, Seren's stomach felt like lead in her body, weighing her down and making her sick.

Can we make it seven? he messaged back. *There's a ton of problems in the dog world right now.*

Seven is fine, she said. To avoid getting sidetracked by Sorrell, Seren made a contingency plan to leave the house at six anyway. Although, last night, Sorrell had only come out to grab a bottle of water and heat a leftover container of spaghetti, which she promptly took back to her bedroom.

At home, she showered and put on a cute pair of denim shorts, a yellow sleeveless top made mostly of cotton and air, and a pair of sandals. She did leave the house at six, after brushing on some blush and mascara, just to avoid anything that might happen.

Seren hated being in avoidance mode. Not only that, she didn't have anywhere to go. She went down the lane to Sarena's house, though she didn't expect her or Darren to be there. The chores around a ranch never ended.

She knocked and opened the front door, the house

spreading before her bright and white and new. "Hello?" she called.

"In the bedroom," Sarena said from the depths of the house. She came out of the hallway several seconds later, her baby bump impossible to miss. A smile entered Seren's soul, and she relaxed for the first time in almost two days. "Hey." She gave Seren a hug. "What are you doing here?" She scanned her. "All dressed up too."

"I had some time to kill before my date," she said. "There's bad energy at the house."

"Ah, of course. Come in. I'm just sorting through some things in the nursery." She led the way back into the bedrooms, and Seren went with her.

"You have a crib and everything."

"Darren built it," she said, smiling fondly at the furniture. "I'm going through some supplies and clothes. There's so much you need for a baby." She shook her head as if this were her worst challenge.

Seren knew it wasn't, and to think so was highly unfair. "How are you feeling?"

"I'm good," she said.

"You hired someone to replace Theo?"

"Yes," Sarena said. "And I cancelled the second position for now." She folded a yellow pair of pajamas that would never fit an actual human being. They were far too small. "I told everyone I'd do interviews in October."

"That gives you a couple more months." Seren watched Sarena nod. Giving up her work on the ranch would be very hard for her, and Seren probably thought her oldest sister was going through a lot of the same things Sorrell was.

Change had never been easy for either of them. Seren just buttoned everything up, bottled it away, pushed it down, and dealt with it never.

They worked together in silence, and Seren realized how much she missed Sarena's presence. When she needed to get back to the farmhouse, where she planned to meet Brian on the front porch, she drew Sarena into a hug. "I love you," she whispered, about as sentimental and emotional as she ever got.

"I love you, too, Seren." Sarena pulled away and searched her face. "Are you okay?"

"Yeah." Seren smiled and nodded. "Yeah, it's just been rough at the farmhouse lately."

"I know. I'm sorry I'm not more helpful."

"We're all doing what we can," Seren said, and she honestly believed that. "I've got to meet Brian. See you later."

"Have fun."

Seren walked the two hundred yards back to the farmhouse and then up the steps, reaching the top just as Brian's truck rumbled toward her. She hurried back to the driveway, and he stopped next to her. She got in, and the air felt like soup. "Hey," she managed to say.

"Hey." He turned around and started back the way he'd come. "Where do you want to go tonight?"

Seren suddenly didn't want to go anywhere with him. "Maybe just pull off up here like we have sometimes."

He threw her a look of surprise. "Really?"

"Yeah."

"Why?" He didn't slow down as their secret meeting place approached.

"Just stop the truck, Brian." She sucked in a breath, and he dang near slammed on the brakes. She gasped, her hand flying out to grab onto the door handle. Instant annoyance shot to the top of her head, and she glared at him.

"I thought we were going to dinner," he said.

"Yeah, and I thought we didn't lie to each other." She leveled her gaze at him. "But you've lied to me, Brian. I know you didn't have a ranch meeting last night."

He blinked, his jaw jumping as he pressed his teeth together.

"Where were you?"

"I prefer not to say right now."

"Are you seeing someone else?"

He gave a mirthless laugh, the chilling nature of it filling the cab with awkwardness that made Seren's skin crawl. "No, not a chance."

"I don't feel like going out with you," she said, dangerously close to tears. She cursed her emotions for welling up now. She sniffed, hoping it didn't sound like a sniffle. At the same time, she wanted to be real with him, and she wasn't a robot. She was allowed to be upset and cry.

"Are you crying?" he asked, pure shock in his voice.

"No," she clipped out.

"I've never seen you get emotional—at least not over...us."

Her fingers scrambled for the door handle. "I'm going to walk back to the farmhouse."

"What did I say?"

She got out of the truck, the man sitting behind the wheel not the Brian Gray she'd started to fall in love with. Fear paralyzed her for a moment. Had she started to love him?

Yes, her mind whispered, and real tears did prick her eyes then. "I already know I'm not emotional, Brian," she said, her voice quivering. "I don't need you to point it out to me."

"Seren—"

"You lied to me," she said, letting her anger drive out her tears. "You prefer not to say where you were. You told me we were okay, but we're not. You said you'd call last night, and you didn't. I was on-edge all day waiting to hear from you, and then I was like, 'reach out to him, Seren. Show him you care about him.' So I did."

"I answered," he said.

She nodded, her emotions bobbing with the movement. "I just...maybe this is just too hard. You can keep your secrets, and I can go comfort my sister, and we'll both just be happier."

Brian simply stared at her, a hard edge in his eyes. "If that's what you want."

It was absolutely not what she wanted, but she also didn't want to get back in the truck and pretend like everything was okay. "Sorry I made you drive over here," she said. "Have a good night."

She slammed the door and walked away from the truck, heading for the road. She went down it a few strides, and then ducked into the trees so that when Brian backed out, he wouldn't be able to see her.

Her breath came too fast. Her chest hurt so much. Her fingers clenched into fists.

Her eyes filled with heartbroken tears, and she let them fall down her face for the first time in a very, very long time.

That cowboy had just driven away with her heart, and Seren suddenly understood Sorrell on a whole new level.

Chapter 23

Brian looked up when Seth answered the door. He wore a wide smile and held an infant in his arms, and everything in Brian's life got better. As good as it could get at the moment, probably.

"You got her," Brian said, smiling at the baby. At the same time, something squeezed inside his chest that hurt like nothing he'd experienced before.

"We did," Seth said, gazing at the baby girl with so much love in his face it actually twisted the knife in Brian's chest. "Come in. You wanted to talk?"

"Yeah." He stepped into the house as Seth fell back and turned to close the door behind him. "What did you name her?"

"Cindy," he said.

"Where's Jenna?"

"She went to get groceries, and more bottle stuff. I don't know. She knows what she wants." He led Brian past the piano studio and into the kitchen. They sat on the couch, and Seth finally looked away from his new daughter. "What's up?"

Brian swiped his cowboy hat off his head, hoping Seth would understand without him having to explain too much. "I've decided it's time for me to move on."

Seth's eyebrows went up, but he didn't say anything.

"I've been here a while, and I don't know. I feel stuck."

"I thought you liked the job."

"I do."

"The dogs are too much?"

"They're not." Brian shook his head and tried to find the right thing to say. "It's nothing to do with you and the others. I really like working here. I like everyone." He was going to miss them so much. His throat narrowed. "Maybe I'm just being irrational."

"Why do you think it's time to move on if you like everyone and the work?" Seth bounced his newborn, and Brian let himself watch him for a few seconds.

"Serendipity broke up with me," he said with a sigh. "I just don't want to be here anymore."

Seth looked down as Cindy made a grunting noise. He seemed to light up from within, and a thread of guilt pulled through Brian that he was bothering Seth on this happy day for him. "I should go. It's not pressing. I haven't even applied anywhere yet."

"You haven't?"

"Theo got on at The Singer Ranch, and I was thinking of applying there. I just haven't pulled the trigger yet." He'd been looking online for a solid week. He didn't know what he was waiting for.

Seren to call, he thought, and that was his answer. Pure misery streamed through him, and he stuffed his hat back on his head and stood up. "I'll be around a while yet, I suppose. I guess I just wanted to let you know what I was thinking."

"Do you see Seren that much around the ranch?" Seth asked, rising as well. "I mean, maybe you just need to let some time go by. Put your head down and do the work, and it'll all go out in the wash, and you'll still be here—where you like everyone and the work." He lifted his eyebrows, so much hope in his eyes. "I'd hate to lose you because of Seren."

"It's not because of Seren," Brian said, though he'd literally just said it was. "It's just...everything. My cabin has no personality. I come home to an empty room." He shook his head. "It's fine."

"I thought you liked living alone. It was crowded in that other cabin."

"I do," Brian said. "I'm aware I'm not making much sense." He put the biggest smile he could muster on his face. "Forget I said anything."

"I'm not going to forget it," Seth said. "It has roots somewhere, Brian."

"Yeah."

Seth cocked his head and looked at Brian with a thoughtful expression. "What are they?"

Brian drew in a breath and held it. "If I'm being honest, and if you won't tell anyone..." He paused and looked at Seth.

"I don't tell anyone anything," Seth said. "You can trust me."

"I do trust you." Brian looked away, the words in his mouth almost like poison. "When things get hard, Seth, I run. That's what I do. It's why I came to the Hill Country in the first place." He looked up. "I sold the apps, and I left Seattle, because my wife had been cheating on me for two years. I ran." The words seared the back of his throat, and he couldn't swallow enough to cool it.

"Maybe it's time to stop running," Seth said.

"Easier said than done, my friend." Brian straightened his hat, a genuine smile barely lifting the corners of his mouth. "I'm still going to look at the job board tonight."

"Okay," Seth said. "But Brian, really think about it. Pray if you do that sort of thing. Don't just run blindly. If you still feel like running with both eyes open, that's different."

"Okay," Brian said. "Thanks, Seth. Congratulations again on the baby." He peered over the pink bundle to see the little girl's face. Cindy looked like an angel straight from heaven, so relaxed and so peaceful. "She's so beautiful."

"Thanks," Seth said. "We're in love with her."

"I bet you are." Brian nodded and added, "I can show myself out." He left, very happy for Seth and Jenna. They'd wanted a baby for a long time, and they'd had some setbacks in their journey toward parenthood.

Maybe that was all he was dealing with with Seren. A setback.

Somehow, he didn't think so. He'd broken up with her twice now, because she chose a vow she'd made with her sister over a relationship with him. There was more to Seren than what she showed people, he knew that. He knew her hesitation at first had more to do with her own insecurities than with Sorrell, but at the very first chance she got, she still chose her sister over him.

"You did lie to her," he said. He hadn't had a ranch meeting, but he hadn't cheated on her either. He'd gone to a job fair in the next town over, though he hadn't applied for a single one. He did secure a username and password to their private job board, and he was going to look at it that night.

He'd forgotten to call her, that was all. He was allowed to forget things, wasn't he? Everyone forgot something at some point in their lives.

She'd brought him coffee, and in the moment she'd asked if they were okay, they were. He'd been surprised by her actions, actually, and he did appreciate that she'd thought of him. She'd texted him first about their date too, and he liked that.

Back in his cabin, he couldn't get himself to call or text Seren, though he wanted to very badly. If he just heard the sound of her voice, everything would be okay. It was much easier to numb his mind—and his heart—by searching for ranch hand or cowboy jobs in the Texas Hill Country area, so he simply did that.

Another week passed, and Brian still didn't apply for any jobs. Thursday night found him next door at the cabin where he used to live with Aaron and Tomas. He went up the back steps, Queen crowding him in the narrow space, and knocked as he juggled the king-size bag of mini candy bars. "Hey," he called as he walked in.

The scent of something spicy and roasted met his nose, and Brian stopped to take a deep breath of it. "Tomas is making tamales," he said, an inkling of joy moving through him. Finally. He hadn't felt happy since Seren had asked him to pull over before they'd even gotten off her ranch.

"That's right," Tomas said from the direction of the stove. "So I hope you're hungry and that you're ready for the spice. The chiles were hot today, boys!" He laughed at the joke inside what he'd said. Brian didn't get it, but he never had with Tomas.

Aaron got up from the table to take the candy bars. "I love these," he said with a big smile. "Darren and Stephen should be here any minute. And they're bringing the new hire from Fox Hollow too."

"Great," Brian said, hoping he'd infused the right amount of excitement into his voice. He did miss Darren now that the other cowboy had jumped the fence to Fox Hollow, and he liked Stephen too. "What's his name?"

"It's a woman," Aaron said. "Becca or Bethany or something with a B."

"It's not a B," Tomas argued. "It's a D. Dani or...Davy."

"Davy?" Brian laughed. "I'm going to go with Aaron on this one, Tomas. You're not great with the consonants that sound the same."

Tomas shrugged, his good nature infectious. Before Brian

could say anything about having a woman at their usually all-male poker night, the front door opened. Darren led the way inside, followed by Stephen, and then a woman with hair the color of a darkened penny.

"Hey, guys," Darren said, shaking Aaron's hand and embracing him with other. He was so happy now too, and Brian envied him powerfully in that moment. "This is Britta."

"Britta," Aaron practically shouted. "With a B." He stepped toward her and shook her hand. "Welcome, welcome. Do you guys have your ante?"

"Stephen's got it all," Darren said, and Aaron took a giant bowl of muddy buddies from Stephen. Brian's mouth watered, and he could skip the tamales and go right for the chocolate and peanut butter covered cereal.

"Let's eat," Tomas said. "Grab a plate. Load up. We'll eat and then play."

Everyone moved then, chatting and laughing in the small space. The noise increased while they got tamales and green salad, moved and shifted chairs around so all six of them could sit at the table for four, and then it got quiet as they ate.

"Where did you come from?" Aaron asked Britta.

She quickly swallowed the last of her tamale and said, "Crested Ridge? It's a drive from here. At least an hour."

"Why'd you come here?" Tomas asked. "Chestnut Springs is tiny."

"My boyfriend moved here," she said with a smile. "Got a job at this family law firm that he says is *amazing*." She half-rolled her eyes.

"Probably Janelle's," Brian said.

"His boss's name is Janelle," Britta said, surprise coating the words. "How did you know?"

"Janelle has the best law firm in these parts," Brian said. He put Crested Ridge in his mind, because maybe they still had a job opening.

"How's Fox Hollow?" Aaron asked.

Britta shot a look at Darren and looked back at Aaron. "Great, I like it." Her voice was far too high to be believable, and Brian watched Darren too.

"What don't you like about it?" he asked evenly.

She exchanged a glance with Stephen, who acted like he'd gone deaf and had no idea what anyone was talking about. "Sarena needs to hire that second person," she finally said. "It's a great ranch, but it needs a lot of work." She nodded like that was that. "If she'd hire another person, we could get it caught up and keep it that way." She nudged Stephen with her elbow. "Tell him what you told me."

Stephen narrowed his eyes at her, finally sighing. "I always feel like we're one step behind. Sometimes five steps. Just when we get something done, there's something else we've neglected, and if we'd have been on top of the problem, it would take less time and energy to fix."

"We just need someone else," Darren said. "Fair enough." He finished his tamale too. "I don't think Sarena liked any of the other candidates, so she paused the hiring."

Brian kept his head down while they talked about hiring someone else at Fox Hollow. That was one job he definitely wasn't going to apply for.

* * *

The next morning, Brian severely regretted the three tamales he'd consumed the night before, as well as the copious amount of muddy buddies. He groaned as his alarm went off, only realizing a moment later that it wasn't his alarm at all.

His phone was ringing.

He sat up and picked up the phone in one motion, finding a local, but unknown, number on the screen. The clock at the top said it was four-fifty. Who in their right mind would be calling him this early in the morning?

He let the call go to voicemail and lay back down. He still had ten minutes before he had to drag himself out of bed, and he wasn't going to do it a moment sooner than necessary. His phone bleeped out the notification that he'd gotten a message, and he swiped to listen to who'd called at this insane hour.

"Brian," a woman said, her voice somewhat familiar. "It's Sarena Adams—Dumond—from next door at Fox Hollow. I realize how early it is, but I thought I'd catch you before you got a start on the ranch. Anyway." She let her voice hang there for a second, and then she said, "Just hear me out, okay? Seren's miserable, and if you like her half as much as she likes you, you probably are too. I need a new ranch hand here at Fox Hollow, and I'm wondering if you want the job."

"What?" he asked, though he was talking to the voicemail.

"Think about it. I'm not opening up to interviews until October, unless you wanted the job."

"Why would I want that job?"

"Okay, that's all. Bye." The message ended, and Brian

hung up without waiting for his options. His mind spun, and he got out of bed and into the shower. He ate, thinking about the message. He went out to the dual dog enclosures, Sarena's voice in his head.

Think about it.

He couldn't *stop* thinking about what his life would be like if he were closer to Seren instead of further from her.

He'd end up like Theo—unless...

"Unless you take the job without telling Seren," he said as he loaded up a huge bag of dog food from the supply shed. "And then show up at the farmhouse and beg her to take you back. Again."

The idea wouldn't leave his mind, and it rotated there like a hurricane, gathering strength with all the additional thought he gave it.

A day passed, and then two. On Sunday, Brian walked into church and sat down to listen to the choir. He didn't even have to start praying. He just knew what he was supposed to do.

Shelve his pride. Take the job. Get Seren back.

When he got home, he sat on the couch with Queen beside him. "Okay," he told her. "Here goes nothing."

Then he dialed Sarena's number.

"Brian," she said pleasantly, as if she'd been expecting him to call all along. "How are you?"

"Nervous," he said, standing up. "I can't believe I called you."

"You're in love with my sister," she said. "I knew you'd call."

He stared at the blank, white walls, her words echoing in his head. *You're in love with my sister.*

He was. He was in love with Serendipity Adams. He cleared his throat. "How do I get her back?"

"We can brainstorm a bit tomorrow," she said, her voice dropping. "Can you come by the ranch during the day while she's at work?"

"Yes." He didn't know how, but he'd figure it out. Seth hadn't been coming to work for the last several days since the adoption, but Brian would figure it out.

"I just have to ask you one thing before I commit to this," Sarena said. "I've already lost a dang good cowboy because of one of my sisters. Is that going to happen again?"

"I think that's a question for Seren," Brian said.

"She's in love with you," Sarena whispered. "She just doesn't know it yet."

Brian didn't dare to even hope that what she'd said was true.

"Tomorrow," she said. "Come after eight and before four. I have to go."

"Okay," he said, but Sarena was already gone. He lowered his phone and looked at Queen. "What just happened?"

He didn't know, and he could hardly wait until tomorrow to find out.

CHAPTER 24

S eren pulled over on the side of the road, the dam inside her head about to break. She couldn't drive and cry at the same time, and she wondered how in the world Sorrell had lived like this her whole life.

She'd made it through a few days of work now since Brian had pulled away from the ranch with her heart held captive. She got up. She smiled at her sister. She'd helped Theo move out. She hiked. She did anything she had to do to stay busy and keep her mind from wandering to the ranch next door.

Her sheer exhaustion had taken over, though, and driving didn't give her enough of a distraction, and she'd allowed herself to think about Brian as she drove home from Enchanted Rock. Big mistake.

Tears spilled down her face, though no sound came out of her mouth. She didn't make a big fuss the way Sorrell did. The tears usually dried up after two or three minutes, but they left her drained beyond belief.

She couldn't believe she even felt this way at all. Every time her phone made any sort of noise at all, her stomach dropped to her shoes. When it came back to where it belonged, that unsettled her too. She was just sure it would be him, and that scared her.

Even worse was thinking that it *wouldn't* be him, and then she'd have to battle with herself over whether she should reach out to him or not. No matter what, she hated feeling like she was about to get caught doing something she didn't want anyone to know about.

She swiped at her eyes, because she didn't want anyone to know she had to pull over and cry on the way home from work.

Serendipity had always been stronger than that.

She thought of her sisters, and how they'd needed her to be the strong one when their father had died. Even Sarena had been utterly distraught then. Seren had been the one to make a lot of the arrangements. She'd called Aunt Scottie and told her the news. She'd written the obituary. She'd done it all without breaking down at all.

She missed her father powerfully in quiet moments, and Seren had learned that if she didn't allow any silence into her life, she didn't have to feel that way.

Without her mother either, Seren felt completely lost in the world. Sarena had so much going on with the ranch and her pregnancy. She only had two more months until her baby boy would be born, and Seren couldn't add to her troubles. Sorrell had turned into a dark-haired zombie who shuffled around the house getting food and filling her coffee cup. She'd stopped cooking, and she'd stopped hanging out with Seren in the living room after work. She had no idea Brian had broken up with Seren, as Seren hadn't told either of her sisters willingly.

Sarena had known something had happened, because she was the most observant sister. She'd come to check on Sorrell the other night, and Seren had been sitting at the bar with a pint of ice cream in front of her. Thankfully, the tears hadn't quite started yet, but Sarena took one look at her and said, "What's wrong?"

Seren had tried to deny it, the same way she'd denied any involvement with Brian Gray last year. As she spoke, she found she didn't have the energy to fend off Sarena, who could fire questions at a person without breathing.

She'd told her, and Sarena had gotten out her own pint of ice cream and joined Seren at the counter. That had been the best night since Brian had driven away, and Seren had answered all kinds of questions—usually her brand of torture.

Sarena had given her space since then, though she had texted to invite her to dinner that night. Seren had said she'd come, because Darren was smoking a brisket. The man knew how to make meat into a morsel, and Seren's stomach growled at her to get going again.

"I need a minute," she said to herself, feeling ridiculous for talking out loud. Everything about this situation was ridiculous, and she encouraged the anger to boil inside her. She much preferred being furious over being sad, and once that anger took over, she'd be able to drive home, shower, and face Sarena and Darren.

She hadn't realized it until Brian was gone, but they were living the life Seren wanted for herself. They had a nice house, with a baby on the way. They wore smiles when they looked at each other, and Darren's quickness to attend to Sarena's every need and want hadn't escaped Seren's attention.

Her fingers tightened on the wheel, and she checked her rear-view mirror to make sure she was clear to ease back onto the road. She could and did, her mind racing around one single idea.

Text him. Text him and tell him you're sorry. Text him. Apologize. Ask him to come over.

Three things. She could accomplish all of them in one text and just a few words. She pressed her teeth together as a defense against pulling over and sending the text right then.

Why shouldn't she?

Trying to answer that question sustained her the rest of the way home, and she parked in front of the house beside Sorrell's car. She didn't anticipate getting the scent of anything cooked when she walked into the farmhouse, so when she smelled a pot roast, she paused.

"Sorrell?" she called, bending to unlace her hiking boots. Her feet ached today, because she'd taken any available shift for the past five days in an effort to make herself so tired she could fall into bed at night and ease directly into sleep.

Sorrell didn't answer, and Seren went down the hall and into the back of the house. As the view widened, she saw a bunch of balloons tied to the back of one of the dining chairs.

A vase of red roses on the counter. A card propped against the vase.

Her heart stopped and so did her feet. When her pulse returned, it sprinted, and she pressed one palm over it to try to soothe it. "Hello?" she asked.

This wasn't for her. Theo had done all of this to try to win over Sorrell. He'd probably been standing in the kitchen with her favorite food—pot roast and mashed potatoes with gravy. They'd made up, and they'd gone outside or back to Theo's old cabin for privacy.

That was definitely what was going on here.

She walked toward the counter anyway, the pristine envelope drawing her attention. It didn't have a name on it, and she picked it up. Flipping it over, she realized it hadn't been opened.

That was very unlike Sorrell, who adored cards and writing little notes to everyone she knew. Even better, she liked receiving them. She would've opened this card.

Seren leaned down to smell the roses, and while she'd never imagined herself getting such a beautiful bouquet of flowers from a man, she now wished she had. No one—not one person—had ever brought her flowers before. Not even Brian.

Happiness for Sorrell moved through her with the flowery scent, and she gazed at the flowers with admiration.

"Okay, so we'll hurry and—shoot."

Seren turned at the sound of her sister's voice. Sarena stood there with a tray of cookies in her oven mitted hands. "She's here," she added over her shoulder. When she looked back at Seren, she asked, "What are you doing home so early?"

"It's after six."

"You said you had the stargazer hike."

"I rolled my ankle on the last hike, and Meg took it for me." Seren barely held back the tears. She'd endured plenty of rolled and sprained ankles in her life. They were annoying, but they'd never brought her to the brink of tears, especially hours later.

Everything in her life felt so hard right now. The littlest of things pushed her toward an edge she'd never been on before.

"I'm sorry," Sarena said, coming into the house, and closing the back door with her foot. She took the tray of cookies to the stovetop and set it down. "Do you want a cookie?"

"Yes," Seren said, sitting on a barstool to give her feet some added relief. "Did Theo bring all this for Sorrell?"

Sarena turned from the stove, two cookies in her hand. "No," she said slowly. She put the cookies on the island in front of Seren. "I made these, so don't get too excited. I think I left out the salt or maybe the vanilla." She smiled at Seren. "Something."

Seren picked up a cookie and bit into it. She got sugar and chocolate, with crispy edges. "It tastes fine," she said.

"Sorrell's would taste delicious," Sarena said. She put one hand on her back and leaned into it. "He's kicking me."

Seren abandoned her cookie and rounded the island to feel the baby. She'd felt him before, and she'd fallen in love with him then. "Did you and Darren decide on a name?"

"No," she said, a frown crossing her face. "We will though."

"I still think Samuel is nice," Seren murmured as the baby kicked again, right against her fingers. "It stays with the S-structure."

"Which is why I don't like it," Sarena said. "Too many S's. I like West, but Darren doesn't think it goes with Dumond."

"West Dumond," Seren said, trying the name out. The baby kicked even harder, and she met Sarena's eye. The hope and joy between them felt like magic, and Seren found herself smiling for the first time in days. "I think he likes it, even if I don't."

Sarena put her hands on her stomach, and Seren slid hers away. "Okay, I have to go," she said. "I was just bringing the cookies." She started for the back door, her footsteps heavy.

Seren looked at the roses again, not wanting to be alone. "Sarena?"

Her sister paused with her hand on the doorknob. "Who's all this for if it's not for Sorrell?"

"You," Sarena said. "Start with the card." With that, she turned the knob and left.

Seren took in the flowers, the card, the balloons, which were all in shades of blue. Light blue. Dark blue. Royal blue. Navy blue. She ran to the back door. "Sarena," she called. "Who was with you earlier?"

She'd definitely spoken to someone, now that Seren thought about it.

"Start with the card," Sarena called over her shoulder, her stride not faltering the tiniest bit.

Seren turned back to the counter, dumbfounded. Her painful feet forgotten, she strode over to the counter where the vase and markless card sat. She picked up the envelope again and used her fingernail to slice through the back of it.

The card inside had a bumpy bouquet of flowers on it, done in watercolor. No words. She took a breath and held it while she opened the card, and those dang tears came back when she saw the obviously male handwriting and her name at the top.

Seren,

I'm in love with you. I can't function without you. You make me so happy, and I want to be a better man because of you.

Please forgive me, and if it's not too late when you get this, and you're not too tired, come to my cabin if you're willing to try just one more time.

Love, Brian

PS. Pop the balloons, even though they're your favorite color.

Tears flowed down her face for the second time that day. A sob caught in her throat. She sank onto the barstool again, wondering what she'd done to deserve the love of a man like Brian.

She was willing to try one more time, and her tears stopped as suddenly as they'd started. She put the card down, rounded the island again, and got out a knife.

Pop! Pop! Pop!

She popped all seven balloons, gathering the little papers that fell from them. She really just wanted to get over to Fox Hollow and rush up his steps. She could apologize then, and tell him she loved him too, and she was definitely willing to try as many times as it took for them to be together.

Her heart pounded at the realizations she made, and her hands trembled as she spread out the papers, quickly realizing it was a puzzle.

She flipped over some pieces, finally getting it all together into a puzzle the size of a piece of paper. Brian had indeed written this on a piece of paper.

"I've moved," she read out loud, flipping the pieces over in a hurry to read what he'd put on the back of the puzzle.

"I'm living closer than before," she said, her eyes trying to skip ahead. "Somewhere you know well. At least you used to. You may not have been there for a while, but all you have to do is take a hop, skip, and a jump from the fairy garden, and you'll find me."

She straightened, her eyes wide. "The fairy garden." She hadn't been out to the circles of rocks and succulents she'd tried to plant as a little girl for years. Probably a decade. Maybe longer.

Only three people knew about that fairy garden, and Brian was not one of them. It was a story she'd never told him, a memory from her childhood with her mother she kept inside of her, because it was so special.

Her father knew about the fairy garden. Sorrell. And— "Sarena."

She left the papers sitting on the table and dashed for the back door. When she stepped onto the super-heated deck, she realized she didn't have shoes on, and she couldn't very well go traipsing out onto the ranch in search of the cabin that sat close to the fairy garden she'd planted for her mother, only a week after her mother's death.

"Dang it," she muttered. She hurried down the hall to her bedroom to find a pair of shoes, jammed them on her feet, and swiped her phone as she passed through the kitchen again.

She needed to get to Brian right now.

CHAPTER 25

Brian paced in the cabin that could seriously use a good scrub from top to bottom. He and Sarena had opened all the windows that morning, and the stale, musty smell was gone now. She'd proven to him that the cabin was habitable by making cookies with ingredients she'd brought over from the homestead.

She'd put dinner together at the farmhouse, though, and he was eternally grateful they'd managed to get the food out of the house before Seren came home.

It had been twenty minutes since he'd jogged around the corner of the house when Sarena had said, "She's here," over her shoulder.

"It's okay," he told himself again. "She'll come." He pressed his palms together and forced himself to take a deep breath. "She's going to come."

He'd laid everything out for her in just a few words inside that card. It had taken him three tries too, and he'd had Sarena proofread it. Every nerve felt exposed, and having his new boss read the deepest feelings of Brian's heart—for her sister—had been very hard for him.

A knock sounded on the door, and Brian spun toward it. His heartbeat shattered through his body, and then Seren asked, "Brian?" from the other side of the door.

He strode toward it, his cowboy boots protecting his feet from the grime on the floor. He'd snuck away from Chestnut Ranch that morning about ten, and he and Sarena had been working on this plan ever since. He had one chance here.

He breathed in and opened the door.

Seren stood there, a high level of anxiety on her face too. She still wore her khaki shorts, issued to her by the Texas Parks Department, and a T-shirt with Enchantment Rock on it.

"You got my card," he said, his voice throaty, as if he hadn't used it enough that day. The complete opposite was true, and he still had miles to go.

"I did," she said. "It was a shame to pop all those balloons."

"They were blue, because you love blue." His brain didn't seem to be lining up the right things for Brian to say. He swallowed, trying to get it to fire right.

She smiled, and that made everything in Brian's life absolutely right. "I do love blue."

"I love you," he blurted. "I can't...I don't want to go through another day, or another hour, or even another minute without you."

"You said that in the card." She nodded to the space behind him. "Can I come in?"

"Yes." He stepped back. "Come in."

She did, glancing around this cabin that had seen better days. "It smells good in here."

"That's our dinner," he said, his fingers lightly brushing hers.

She slid her hand into his and turned toward him. "It's bigger than your other place."

"Yes, it is." He gazed at her, ready to tell the whole story.

Before he could start, she opened her mouth and said, "I love you, Brian. I've cried more in the past few days than I have in my whole life, and I've lost both of my parents." Her eyes turned glassy right then. "I'm sorry. I won't put Sorrell above you."

He nodded, because he believed her. His soul hummed with the words *I love you, Brian.* He could feel it streaming from her, and it was the most wonderful feeling in the world.

"I went to a job fair that night I said I had a ranch meeting," he said.

"A job fair?"

"Yeah." He wanted to kiss her, but maybe she needed the whole story first. "Theo found another job, far from here, because he couldn't really stand to be around Sorrell anymore. It's not because he doesn't want to be. He does. It's all he thinks about." Brian sighed and pulled her closer to him. "I haven't talked to him about it; I just know, because it's how I felt. I wanted to be with you, but I felt like it was impossible. It's a terrible feeling to love someone and think they don't love you back."

"It's not true," she said.

"I know that," he said. "But at the time, I thought I should get another job too. One that put some distance between us. Then maybe I wouldn't be tormented with thoughts of coming to see you, only to have you push me away."

"I didn't mean to do that."

"I know that."

Tears filled her eyes, and to his great surprise, she let them slide down her face. He reached up and wiped them away with his thumb. "Don't cry, sweetheart."

"I feel terrible that I hurt you."

"I lied to you."

She wrapped her arms around him, and they held each other tight. "I'm not going to do that again, Seren," he promised. "Okay? I won't ever lie to you again."

"I will always put you first," she said, tipping her head back to look at him. With tears clinging to her eyelashes, and love filling her gaze, Brian believed her.

He lowered his mouth to hers and kissed her, his definition of joy rewriting itself to mean this moment, right here with her, in what hopefully would become the home where they'd live together, raise a family, and grow old together.

* * *

"Okay, that's it," Seren said, stepping back from the trim she'd just finished painting. "I think it looks amazing, Brian." She looked at him over her shoulder, a glow coming from her. "What do you think?"

"I agree," he said, taking in the light blue paint on the

walls. It played well with the stark white she'd slathered on the ceiling and the trim. The kitchen cabinets were also bright white, and Seren had insisted the kitchen table and chairs should be too.

They'd been working on this cabin for two solid months. They didn't come every evening, because they both had busy jobs and a lot going on. But when they worked on it, it was together. He'd asked her about marriage and family, and she'd admitted she didn't know if she felt like she could be a good mother. He hadn't known what to tell her, but he'd reminded her that she had plenty of feelings, and she'd probably know what to do.

After that, they'd discussed everything from flooring to paint to window treatments. He'd told her he didn't want a stark cowboy cabin without personality. He wanted to make a home for her and with her.

This cabin was bigger than the one at Chestnut Ranch, as it had three bedrooms. Just a single bath, but it would do for now. A kitchen with more counter space than Brian knew what to do with, and a living room that could hold more than one couch.

Not only that, but Brian wanted to build a second floor onto the cabin, or expand off the back of it for more room. A second living area, another bedroom, more bathrooms. Seren hadn't told him no once, but he hadn't lined anything up yet.

He hadn't asked her to marry him yet, and even when he did, it would likely be several months before that happened. They didn't need the extra room for a family right away, though Brian felt like he wanted to press down hard on the accelerator almost all the time.

"Once this is all dry, we can get everything loaded in," she said.

"Perfect." He moved to her side and put his arm around her. "I'll call everyone and arrange deliveries starting on Monday." He pressed a kiss to her temple. "Thank you for painting it for me."

She snuggled into his side, and Brian thought of the diamond he had concealed in a drawer in his bedroom. He'd been trying to think of the perfect time, place, and way to ask her to be his wife, but nothing had come to mind. He needed the help of Sarena for stuff like this, but she was one breath away from delivering a baby. Brian also wanted to come up with romantic things by himself, because he couldn't go running to Seren's sister every time he wanted to impress his girlfriend.

Her phone rang, and she slipped it out of her pocket without going too far from him. "Hey, Sorrell." She pulled in a breath and spun back to him. "Right now?"

He knew immediately what was going on: Sarena was in labor.

"And you're just calling? We won't even make it before he's born." She flapped her hand wildly toward the door, and he swiped his keys from the kitchen table. He followed her out the front door and to his truck as she continued to fire questions at her sister.

"Okay, be there soon." She hung up and reached to put

her seatbelt on, though he'd been driving for a minute already. "Sarena is having the baby."

"I figured."

"Sorrell waited a half an hour to call," she said sourly. "She's been there this whole time, but she knew we were finishing the painting tonight."

"I'm sure we'll make it."

"She said they didn't even leave the ranch until Sarena was having contractions every ninety seconds, and when they got there, she was dilated to a five." She glared out the windshield. "Can you drive really fast, please? I don't want to miss it."

"You're not going into the room, are you?"

"No, but Darren said we could watch the first bath through the glass." She looked at Brian, pure agony in her eyes. "Why didn't she call me? If I miss it, I'm going to be so mad at her."

"We won't miss it," Brian said, pushing down on the gas pedal. He got Seren to the hospital in Chestnut Springs as quickly as he could, and she jogged ahead of him inside. The ride to the third floor maternity wing seemed to take forever, and she clawed her way out of the elevator before the door opened all the way.

Brian did his best to keep up with her, and when he saw Sorrell sitting in a chair, bent over her knees as she looked at her phone, he knew they hadn't missed it.

Seren said something to her sister in an angry tone, and Sorrell stood up. "I'm sorry," she said. "I should've called sooner." She shot a glance in Brian's direction. "I didn't want to interrupt you."

"Has she had him?" Seren asked.

"Not that I've heard. The windows for the nursery are right there." She indicated a bank of glass several feet down the hall. "I check every few minutes, and I haven't seen him or Darren. Besides, Darren said he'd come get us."

In that moment, Darren poked his head out of a nearby door. "We're giving him the bath."

"Darren," Seren practically yelled. "What did you name him? Is Sarena okay?"

"She did amazing," Darren said, his whole face a smile. "We decided to name him West. Go watch." He indicated the windows and ducked back inside.

"Sarena got her way," Seren said. She turned back to Brian and reached for him, pure light on her face. "Come watch, Bri."

He went with her, because he wanted to be by her side through everything. They arrived in front of the windows, and Darren held up a tiny human being with a dark shock of hair on his head.

"Oh, he's beautiful," the sisters said together. Brian squeezed Seren's hand, and she squeezed back. They watched Darren and the nurses give baby West his first bath, the infant not too happy about it, though he never opened his eyes.

Once he was dry and swaddled again, Darren took him through the door in the back corner of the room. Seren turned away from the windows. "I can't wait to hold him."

Brian turned to find a seat, because he had a feeling they were going to be there for a while until Seren could see her sister. Darren came through the door again, this time with the baby.

"You don't have to wait," Brian said. "He's right there."

Seren released his hand and hurried toward Darren. She took the baby from him, her head bent down. Brian arrived at her side as she whispered, "I love you, West." She looked up at Brian, tears in her eyes.

"I think I can be a mom," she said, her eyes brimming with tears. "Look at him, Brian. Isn't he wonderful?"

The baby grunted, and it was the cutest sound Brian had ever heard. "Yeah," he said. "He sure is."

Hours later, after Seren had gone back to see Sarena and after they'd arrived back at Fox Hollow Ranch, Brian made an excuse to go down the hall to his bedroom. He gathered the diamond ring and took it into the living room.

Seren sat at the table, looking at her phone. "I better get going," she said, standing up while he dropped to one knee. "I have to work in—oh." She'd looked at him, and her eyes widened as the seconds passed.

He held out the jewelry box, which he'd cracked open to reveal the diamond ring inside. "Will you marry me?" That wasn't really the speech he'd been hoping to give, but the words got the job done.

Seren looked from him to the ring and back. A smile burst onto her face. "Yes."

Brian started to laugh, and Seren did too. He stood and put the ring on her finger, his hands stumbling a little along hers. "I love you, Serendipity," he said.

"I love you too, Brian."

He kissed her then, this woman who'd caught his attention over a year ago. There were no more secrets between them, and Brian couldn't wait to make her his wife.

* * *

In **A COWBOY AND HIS SKIPPED CHRISTMAS**, you'll get to see if Theo will stay away from Sorrell, or if she'll track him down at his new ranch... Keep reading for a sneak peek!

SNEAK PEEK! CHAPTER ONE OF A COWBOY AND HIS SKIPPED CHRISTMAS

Theo Lange swung down from the huge chestnut bay he rode, reaching for his gloves in the next moment. Life certainly wasn't dull at The Singer Ranch, but Theo could use an afternoon where he didn't sweat through his clothes as he literally chased errant cattle.

"Ho, there," he called, stepping up onto the bottom rung of the fence. He waved one arm above his head to the two or three cowboys in the field.

A couple of dogs barked, and that got everyone to turn and look at Theo. He balanced and waved both hands above his head in the sign he'd learned to indicate they had livestock on the loose.

The three men swung toward him, one of them—probably Jake—whistling at the cattle canines they used. The blue heelers streaked toward Theo, and he did absolutely love them.

He didn't love much else about this operation. Robert Singer was a tough, old man, and he did not mince words.

Theo had witnessed him dress down one of the best cowboys on the ranch, then lay into the foreman, and then press one hand against his son's chest when Ben had tried to intervene.

Theo had stood there in complete shock, wishing he could make himself smaller just in case Robert's attention somehow zeroed in on him. When the old cowboy had turned toward the line of guys, Theo had dropped his eyes to the ground and hid his face with the wide brim on his cowboy hat.

He got back in the saddle on a horse he'd named Bear, because all horses should have names. He'd learned that none of the horses here had names, and that was just unacceptable to Theo.

The dogs had names, and they seemed open to the constant stream of people moving on and off the ranch. Theo had made better friends with them than anyone else on the ranch in the last two months since he'd been here.

"They've broken through that temporary fence on Road Twelve," he said as the other cowboys joined him. The dogs streaked ahead of them, and Theo moved his horse into a trot to follow the others.

He wasn't as good with a rope as they were, because he didn't spend his days in a saddle, throwing ropes, and herding cattle back where they belonged. He missed Fox Hollow with a fierceness he'd thought he'd been ready for.

He had not been ready. He had never in a million years thought he'd be this miserable. He slept on the bottom bunk in a shared bedroom, with two more cowboys across the hall. The four of them shared a tiny bathroom, and Theo barely had time to grab a few swallows of coffee before he left the cabin bright and early.

Since he was the last one who'd come to The Singer Ranch in his cabin, he was the low man on the totem pole. He showered last. He got the dregs of the coffee. The ends of the bread.

As he rode behind the others, Theo wondered how his life had come to this moment.

You don't need this job, he thought. He didn't need the job, and his desire to quit pulled through him with utmost strength.

He did not want to be here anymore.

His bank account had plenty of money in it, and he wanted his own house. He could get a couple of his own horses, name them what he wanted, and get a pair of dogs to go with them.

He'd thought he wanted to hide, and he'd never been much for displaying how much money he had. At this point, he'd take a one-bedroom cabin where he got up and made his own coffee and then scrambled his own eggs.

He veered to the left to head off the cattle making a turn that way. His thoughts would not be distracted though, and he couldn't believe how good his life had been at Fox Hollow.

An image of Sorrell Adams filled his mind, blocking out the black beef cows trying to make his life difficult. He yipped at them, and Bluebell barked at the cattle, sending them back toward Roland, Jake, and Sam.

By the time they got the cattle contained, Theo had made up his mind.

He was done at The Singer Ranch. At this point, he'd

leave behind everything he'd brought with him. He just wanted to get in his truck and go to the first hotel he could find.

That wasn't entirely true. He wanted to go to the first hotel he could find that had an on-site restaurant, room service, and air conditioning.

He brushed down his horse, finished his chores, and walked over to the administration building. It was one of the newer buildings on the ranch, and a blast of cool air hit him in the face when he entered.

Thanksgiving would arrive next week, but Texas hadn't seemed to have gotten the memo yet, and the sun still super-heated everything under its broad face.

"Hey, Courtney," Theo said, tipping his hat to the woman. "Is Winn at his desk?"

"He just went over to the barn office."

Theo pivoted, determined to talk to Winn today. The thought of waking up in the morning and working through another twelve hours, with people he didn't know, and no connection to anyone or anything had his chest tightening immensely.

He left his truck in front of the administration building and strode toward the barn. He went in the side door and turned into the office, relief flooding him when he saw Winn standing at his desk.

He glanced up from the computer. "Hey, Theo," Winn said.

"Hey." Theo took a deep breath. "Listen, I know this

could cause a problem for you, but I just can't do this anymore."

Winn stopped typing on the keyboard and looked up fully. "I thought you were a career cowboy."

Theo pressed his teeth together and reminded himself that yes, that was the persona he'd put forward for the past several years. "I just need a change," he said. "I thought a new ranch would do it, but I was wrong."

He hated the work here, and his fingers twitched to be on his way.

"All right," Winn said. "I hate to lose you. You're one of the hardest workers we've had."

"I appreciate that," Theo said. "I'm really sorry."

"It's okay," Winn said. He reached for something in the desk. He'd built it himself, and Theo liked the standing desk, which had a sloped top to hold Ben's computer, and a few drawers down the front of it.

He took out a paper and handed it to Theo. Their eyes met, and Theo could almost see a mirror of his dark eyes in the brown depth's of Ben's.

He worked all the time, despite being married with children. Theo had never seen him in anything but a pair of jeans, cowboy boots, a button-down shirt in a variety of patterns and colors, and that cream-colored cowboy hat.

Theo wished he wanted to be as predictable. He hated routine, though, and as he stood there and listened to Winn talk about the paper he wanted Theo to sign to terminate his employment at The Singer Ranch, Theo started planning his vacation.

"Where are you going to go now?" Winn asked, handing the pen to Theo.

He signed his name, and said, "I don't know." He glanced up at the man who had hired him. "I'll just get my next paycheck via direct deposit?"

"Sure thing," Winn said, already back to his computer.

Theo's phone beeped at him, and he really wanted to see what that notification was from his Dow Jones app. He only had specific ones set, and it must be an important one.

"Thanks," Theo said, and he ducked out of the barn office. He checked his phone, and the price of Continental had reached the high he'd set.

He didn't even have time to walk back to his truck. He moved fast, because the clock was ticking in New York. Six minutes until the Dow closed, and Theo needed to get rid of Continental right now.

In the morning, everyone would be trying to unload, and the stock price would fall. He'd learned from his father to be ruthless when it came to selling. He couldn't hold onto stocks because he hoped they'd do something.

They're predictable, Theodore, his dad used to say. *Buy low. Sell high. Set a limit, and when it's reached, sell. Don't wait.*

Don't hesitate.

Theo didn't hesitate, and he quickly tapped a few times, finally touching the green SELL button and confirming it.

Three minutes to spare, and the six thousand shares of Continental left his account. He sighed as he leaned against the wall, then he got himself out of the barn and back to the microscopic cabin where he'd been living for the last couple of months.

He'd shown up with a couple of suitcases, and he left with the same, his roommates just watching him. "You're leaving?" Martin asked.

"Yes," Theo said, putting a smile on his face. Standing there, he realized how unhappy he was.

"Going somewhere else?" Kent asked.

"Not another ranch, no," Theo said. He quickly ran through his list of belongings, telling himself he could literally buy anything he left behind. A new toothbrush, a pair of boots, a set of plates. None of it mattered.

"It's been great," he lied, keeping his smile hitched in place. The others responded likewise, and Theo made his exit from The Singer Ranch without fanfare.

As he drove away, the heavy relief filling him did buoy his mood.

He hated this time of year, and he really just wanted to skip the holidays completely. His father had died the day before Christmas, and Theo did his best to participate in as few holiday events as possible.

This year, without anywhere to belong, he could skip Christmas completely.

The idea appealed to him like nothing else had, and with the sale of his Continental stock, he'd just made almost a million dollars.

He could skip anything he wanted.

He drove to Austin and pulled over to search for the nicest hotel he could find. Then he went down a couple of steps and navigated to a three-and-a-half star hotel that had a pool, suites, the restaurant he wanted, and bonus—a park right across the street.

Theo's gratitude doubled when he asked for a suite and they had one. He showered in hot water for the first time in months, sighing as he did.

He put on gym shorts and a T-shirt, left his cowboy hat in his suite, and headed down to the restaurant. He needed a steak to celebrate his freedom from The Singer Ranch, and that would give him enough energy to check his stocks, plan a day at the park tomorrow, and then figure out where he should go so he could leave Christmas behind this year.

Downstairs, he stepped to the podium, the lights inside the restaurant dim and the music low. "Do I need a reservation?" he asked.

"No, sir," the woman drawled, glancing up. "Are you a guest here?" She wore a pretty smile, and Theo finally felt like he had enough energy and reason to return it.

"Yes." His pulse did nothing when looking at this woman, though he supposed she was attractive. The problem was, his heart had been beating for Sorrell Adams—and only Sorrell Adams—for so long, he wasn't even sure if he'd recognize attraction to another woman.

"Do you want me to put the charges on your room?" she asked.

"Sure." He gave her his room number, and she turned to take him to a table. He'd taken one step when a woman to his left and behind him said, "Theo?"

He knew who he'd see even as he turned his head toward

the woman that had been torturing him since the day he started at Fox Hollow Ranch.

"Sorrell," he said, drinking her in. She'd curled that gorgeous hair so it fell in loose waves over her shoulders. She wore makeup so well that it enhanced her natural beauty, and she looked like she'd just come from a meeting.

He noticed that she stood with someone, and Theo looked to him.

His chest tightened again, and he didn't want to hear her introduce him to her new boyfriend. She'd refused him so many times, and he could not stand the thought of her going out with someone else.

"Good to see you," he said, his voice tight. He turned to follow the hostess, ramming right into the podium. Pain shot through his ribs and down into his stomach, and he couldn't stop the grunt as it flew from his mouth.

Humiliation flowed through him now, and he shot a glance at Sorrell, who still stood there with her new cowboy boyfriend, and Theo dodged the podium and walked away as fast as he could.

Sneak peek! Chapter Two of A Cowboy and his Skipped Christmas

Sorrell Adams stared after the only man she wanted to talk to. The only man she wanted to be with.

Her heart hammered in her chest, and every cell in her body seemed to be vibrating. She pulled in breath after breath, her mind racing as she tried to figure out what to do.

"You better go after him," Lance said.

"Should I?" Sorrell asked, looking at her secretary. She hated this weakness in her, but her eyes had already started to fill with tears.

The last two months had been some of the hardest of her life, and she honestly thought she'd never see Theo Lange again.

Why was he here?

Was God trying to play some trick on her? She hadn't been to Austin in years, and the one time she was here for training on a new software system, she ran into Theo Lange?

She pressed one hand to her heart, still at a complete loss as to what to do.

"Let's go," Lance said, actually taking her hand and towing her toward the podium. The woman that Theo had been talking to returned to the podium, and she glanced at them.

"Two?"

"Actually, no," Lance said, and Sorrell was glad he was taking charge. She felt like a fool, but right now, she needed him. That was their professional relationship. She helped him sometimes, and sometimes he assisted her.

She'd never shared much of her personal life with him, but Lance had eyes, and he'd obviously seen something between Sorrell and Theo.

"She just needs to sit with that man you just took back." Lance leaned into the podium and put a dashing smile on his face. "And I need to know what time you get off."

"Oh, my word," Sorrell said, staring at him now. How could he say things like that? She couldn't even imagine having that kind of confidence.

The woman giggled and said, "I'm not off until midnight, sir." She glanced at Sorrell. "And he's in a booth, so there's room for you."

Sorrell could never walk through the restaurant and slide into the booth across from Theo.

"I'll take her back," Lance said, still smiling for all he was worth. He knocked a couple of times on the podium, seized her hand again, and took her with him.

"No," she said, trying to dig in her heels, but the floor in this place was smooth and shiny. "I can't."

"You can," Lance said, easily towing her along. "And you will."

"You don't even know who he is," Sorrell said.

"Sure I do," Lance said. "He's Theo, and he's the one you think about when I catch you staring at nothing in your office."

Sorrell didn't even know she'd been doing that. She had been quite unfocused at work since Theo's departure from the ranch, because she'd lost her whole support system when he'd left her life.

"Sir," Lance said, pouring Southern charm into his tone now. "We overbooked, and this lovely lady needs a seat. You have one, so we're going to put her right here with you."

Sorrell met Theo's gaze, and though she could hardly see in only the low light stuck to the wall on the inside of the booth, she definitely saw something flash in Theo's eyes.

She wasn't sure if it was anger or desire. He could easily look around and see this restaurant was practically empty, but he nodded to the other side of the table. "She took the other menu."

"Oh, Sorrell doesn't eat a whole lot," Lance said easily. He almost shoved Sorrell into the booth. "Our meetings don't start until ten, but that doesn't mean you can stay out too late tonight." He flicked his gaze to Theo. "Boss."

With that, Lance walked away, and Sorrell swore she heard him chuckle to himself.

She sat in the booth, quivering in front of the one person she'd always been the most comfortable with, and she hated that.

When he'd left, she'd lost so much.

Tell him, she thought.

Seren had been telling her to just text Theo and tell him how she felt. Her sister wanted Sorrell to ask Theo out, but Sorrell didn't know how to do that. She didn't understand the order the words needed to be in.

"What are you doing here?" he asked, his focus completely on the menu.

"New software training," she said.

"How long will you be here?"

"Through Sunday." Sorrell had nothing to look at and nothing to occupy her hands. She could look at Theo's handsome face all day and all night, and right now, she was staring at him.

He hadn't been shaving at his new ranch, and Sorrell rather liked the full beard and mustache. He wasn't wearing a cowboy hat tonight, and he looked so...normal.

"What about you?" she asked, hating the formalities between them.

"I'm undecided," he said.

"Undecided?"

He finally looked up and passed her the menu, his eyes skating all over the place. "Yes. Undecided."

"What does that mean?"

"I think you'll like the egg roll appetizers," he said, and

Sorrell felt like they were having four different conversations. She wouldn't be able to eat much at all, not with the way her stomach was currently shrieking at her.

"Something to drink?" the waiter asked. "You don't have a menu."

"It's fine," Theo said. "I've looked, and I know what I want."

So he wasn't undecided about his food. Sorrell frowned at the scarcity of items on the menu, and she looked up as Theo ordered a diet cola.

"Same," she said.

"Ready to order?"

"Yes," Theo said. "I want the sirloin, medium-rare, please."

The waiter nodded and said, "The market price on that is sixty-seven dollars."

"Fine," Theo said, and they both looked at her.

Sixty-seven dollars for steak and mashed potatoes? Sorrell just blinked.

"She'll have the egg roll appetizers," Theo said. "As a meal, and she wants the beet and goat cheese salad. I'm guessing on the raspberry vinaigrette?" He raised his eyebrows, and Sorrell had the wherewithal to nod.

Theo nodded too, and so did the waiter, and with all that nodding going on, Sorrell finally found her voice.

"Where are you working now?" she asked, handing the waiter the menu so he could walk away.

"I'm not," he said. "I quit my job today. That's why I'm here."

"Oh." So many more questions began streaming through her head, but Sorrell couldn't latch on to only one for long enough to speak it.

The waiter returned with their drinks, and Theo calmly unwrapped his straw. He wasn't offering up any other conversation handholds, and awkwardness raced through Sorrell.

"What are your plans?" she asked. Chestnut Springs was having a bachelor auction next week, and she needed more men. Maybe Theo...

Suddenly, the thought of anyone else going out with him revolted her.

"I have no plans," he said. "Right now. I'm going to plan a vacation when I go back to my room."

"I know Seth Johnson is looking for a couple of guys at Chestnut," she said. That would keep Theo close, and Sorrell began to wonder if they could simply go back to the way things used to be between them.

"I'll call him," Theo said, picking up his glass to take a drink.

"I miss you," she blurted out, her emotions surging. "I hate that I don't see you every day, and I hate that I lost my best friend."

Theo froze, his glass of cola halfway to his mouth. It seemed to take great effort for him to lift his eyes to meet hers, and Sorrell's hands shook as she reached for her own drink.

"Come back, Theo," she said. "Even if you can't come to Fox Hollow, come to Chestnut. You'll be close, and I'll ask you out a hundred times. Two hundred times—until you say yes."

She had no idea where the words had come from. Perhaps they had existed inside her all this time, and she simply hadn't realized it.

What was more true was probably that she'd simply been terrified to let them out of the box where she'd been storing them. Sorrell had spent a lot of time afraid of a lot of things.

She didn't want to do that anymore, especially with Theo.

"So if you come back," she said when he remained silent. "Would you go to dinner with me?"

He finally continued the trajectory of his glass and took a sip of his soda through the straw. "We're at dinner together right now."

"So you wouldn't go out with me again?"

"Depends."

"On what?"

"On how well this date goes," he said, stirring the straw around and making the ice cubes clink against the glass. "That's how dating works, Sorrell. If the first date goes well, you ask for a second one."

"Is this a first date then?"

He lifted one powerful shoulder in a shrug. "Up to you."

"No," she said. "I don't want things to be up to me." She made so many decisions at work as it was. She just wanted someone to tell her what to do with the rest of her life.

Seren had tried to tell Sorrell exactly what to do—*ask him*. She could practically hear her sister's voice in her ears right then.

She had asked him.

He hadn't come right out and said yes. She suddenly knew how much courage it took to ask someone out, and how nerve-racking it was when they acted like they didn't want to go.

She'd not only acted like that, but she'd rejected him so many times.

"Did Sarena have her baby?" Theo asked, and Sorrell's whole soul lit up.

"Yes," she said. "She did."

"What did she name him?"

"West," she said. "He's so great, Theo." Sorrell didn't want to emit a wistful sigh, but it was very hard work to hold it back.

"I bet he is." Theo smiled then, and it was so devastatingly handsome that Sorrell let out a different kind of sigh. To get a grip on herself, she too reached for her straw and busied herself with her soda.

"Where did you go?" she asked.

"The Singer Ranch," he said, and the conversation picked up from there. Before she knew it, Sorrell and Theo had fallen right back into their old ways.

She could tease him, and he'd laugh. He could say something serious to her, and she'd watch him to make sure she knew how he felt about something.

She knew one thing—she really liked Theo, and she'd been an absolute idiot by refusing him for so long that he wouldn't ask again.

Finally, he tossed some money on the table, and they slid out of the booth. It was likely way past Sorrell's bedtime, but she felt like she'd been hooked to an IV filled with energy drinks.

"I've been waiting for you to ask me out again," she said, linking her arm through his. "I was going to say yes." She looked up at him, but he didn't meet her eye. "You didn't ask again."

"A man can only hear no so many times," he murmured.

"I'm sorry," she said. "I was in a bad place for so long, and that put you in a bad place, and it just never lined up."

They went to the elevators to the left of the restaurant, and he put in his keycard to be able to call the car.

"Apology accepted," he said, but he did not offer her his arm again or take her hand in his. They got on the elevator together, and she pushed the nine while he pressed the twenty-seven.

"Wow," she said. "Staying on the top floor."

He gave her that smile again, and she wondered if he practiced it in the mirror at night. He had to, because it was so perfect. "Yes," he said. "I rented a suite, because I might be here a while."

Sorrell wanted to know why. She wanted to know how he could afford to stay in a hotel this nice for "a while."

She also did not want to get off on the ninth floor without knowing when she'd see him again, and he still had not accepted any of her invitations.

The elevator dinged on nine, and Sorrell looked at Theo. Theo gazed down at her.

Sorrell did the very first thing that came to her mind. She stepped into Theo's personal space, ran her fingers up

the sides of his face, and drew him down to her level for a
kiss.

* * *

**A Cowboy and his Skipped Christmas is available in
paperback!** Read now to find out what happens after this
kiss...

Chestnut Ranch Romance

Book 1: A Cowboy and his Neighbor: Best friends and neighbors shouldn't share a kiss...

Book 2: A Cowboy and his Mistletoe Kiss: He wasn't supposed to kiss her. Can Travis and Millie find a way to turn their mistletoe kiss into true love?

Book 3: A Cowboy and his Christmas Crush: Can a Christmas crush and their mutual love of rescuing dogs bring them back together?

Book 4: A Cowboy and his Daughter: They were married for a few months. She lost their baby...or so he thought.

Book 5: A Cowboy and his Boss: She's his boss. He's had a crush on her for a couple of summers now. Can Toni and Griffin mix business and pleasure while making sure the teens they're in charge of stay in line?

Book 6: A Cowboy and his Fake Marriage: She needs a husband to keep her ranch...can she convince the cowboy next-door to marry her?

Book 7: A Cowboy and his Secret Kiss: He likes the pretty adventure guide next door, but she wants to keep their relationship off the grid. Can he kiss her in secret and keep his heart intact?

Book 8: A Cowboy and his Skipped Christmas: He's been in love with her forever. She's told him no more times than either of them can count. Can Theo and Sorrell find their way through past pain to a happy future together?

BLUEGRASS RANCH ROMANCE

Book 1: Winning the Cowboy Billionaire: She'll do anything to secure the funding she needs to take her perfumery to the next level...even date the boy next door.

Book 2: Roping the Cowboy Billionaire: She'll do anything to show her ex she's not still hung up on him...even date her best friend.

Book 3: Training the Cowboy Billionaire: She'll do anything to save her ranch...even marry a cowboy just so they can enter a race together.

Book 4: Parading the Cowboy Billionaire: She'll do anything to spite her mother and find her own happiness...even keep her cowboy billionaire boyfriend a secret.

Book 5: Promoting the Cowboy Billionaire: She'll do anything to keep her job...even date a client to stay on her boss's good side.

Book 6: Acquiring the Cowboy Billionaire: She'll do anything to keep her father's stud farm in the family...even marry the maddening cowboy billionaire she's never gotten along with.

Book 7: Saving the Cowboy Billionaire: She'll do anything to prove to her friends that she's over her ex...even date the cowboy she once went with in high school.

Book 8: Convincing the Cowboy Billionaire: She'll do anything to keep her dignity…even convincing the saltiest cowboy billionaire at the ranch to be her boyfriend.

Texas Longhorn Ranch Romance

Book 1: Loving Her Cowboy Best Friend: She's a city girl returning to her hometown. He's a country boy through and through. When these two former best friends (and ex-lovers) start working together, romantic sparks fly that could ignite a wildfire... Will Regina and Blake get burned or can they tame the flames into true love?

Book 2: Kissing Her Cowboy Boss: She's a veterinarian with a secret past. He's her new boss. When Todd hires Laura, it's because she's willing to live on-site and work full-time for the ranch. But when their feelings turn personal, will Laura put up walls between them to keep them apart?

About Emmy

Emmy is a Midwest mom who loves dogs, cowboys, and Texas. She's been writing for years and loves weaving stories of love, hope, and second chances. Learn more about her and her books at www.emmyeugene.com.

Printed in Great Britain
by Amazon